Have you signed up for my newsletter yet?

I send out exclusive sneak peeks of all my new releases and giveaways plus a monthly newsletter where we can get to know each other. I'd love to have you. And, as a special thank you for being a part of my News Friends, I will send you a link to download a FREE eBook copy of my novella, *Of Walls*. You can sign up here: http://eepurl.com/cfqP5H

Also by Sara L. Foust

ROMANTIC SUSPENSE:
LOVE, HOPE AND FAITH SERIES

Callum's Compass: Journey to Love

Camp Hope: Journey to Hope

Rarity Mountain: Journey to Faith

SMOKY MOUNTAIN SUSPENSE
SERIES

The Kidnapping of Cody Moss (Smoky Mountain Suspense Book One)

Women's fiction

Of Walls

THE VANISHING OF OLIVIA BECK

Smoky Mountain Suspense Book
Two

Sara L. Foust

The Vanishing of Olivia Beck, Smoky Mountain Suspense Book Two

©2019 Sara L. Foust

Published by Silver Lining Literary Services
106 Offutt Rd.
Clinton, TN 37716
www.saralfoust.com

Printed in the United States of America

ISBN 978-1-7329047-2-9

Scripture quoted is from the King James Version of the Bible, which is in public domain.
©2019 Cover Design by Sara L. Foust

For Emma

My quirky, kind second born. I love how deeply you feel life and how much you care about others. I love your creativity and your clever wit and your strong will. Never compromise what you believe is best for you. Stay fierce, my brave, independent, beautiful warrior.

And we know that all things work together
for good to them that love God, to them who
are called according to *his* purpose.

Romans 8:38 KJV

Chapter One

Olivia Beck pulled her gaze from the rearview mirror for the tenth time in as many minutes. She would not cry. Not again. Not now.

It was too late for tears. Or too early, she couldn't really say. But her mind was made up, and there was only one way to proceed. Everything was ready, and her plan was set. She gritted her teeth and forced a smile. "Look, Andi! Look, Drew! See the doe over in the field?"

Her daughter and son clambered to be the first to spot the creature. Halfway through the Cades Cove Scenic Loop, and Olivia had already been able to point out a dozen deer and two dozen turkeys.

Could Jonah tell she was off today? That she was trying too hard to seem calm and normal?

She shook her head. Why should she worry about that? Her training had taught her so well, he'd only see if she wanted him to. And she couldn't let that happen. She loved him too much. *Lord, you know what's happening. Where's the bear we discussed?*

"I'm sorry you haven't gotten your shot yet, Livvy." Jonah squeezed her hand.

How she longed to grip it with all her strength and never let go. "We still have time."

"Maybe on the back side with all the blackberry bushes."

"Maybe." She'd love to get "the shot" she'd been wanting for years to add to her collection. But, even if she did today, it would never be added to her bedroom wall with the others. It wasn't even her bedroom wall anymore.

She choked back a rising sob. Stop it, Olivia. This line of thought isn't helping you be strong.

They rounded the curve past the bathrooms and swung into the far side. Her heart picked up speed. She was almost there. Whether she wanted to or not, her gaze traveled to the mirror and took in every detail of her babies' faces. Not that she didn't know them by heart already. Would she eventually forget the contours of their smiles?

A tear leaked from her eye. She swiped it away before anyone could see.

This was exactly why she never wanted to get close to anyone. What had she been thinking?

An opening in the trees led the road toward a wide field. She followed the other motorists in a slow line, half-heartedly listening to the kids' excited chatter in the backseat. She and Jonah didn't need to speak with idle words. She would miss that.

"There!" Jonah leaned forward and pointed to a tall tree. "See it?"

Her heart rate spiked. In the top of the branches, a large, black form appeared between the leaves. There was the bear she'd specifically asked God to send.

It was time.

She pulled onto the shoulder and took a deep breath.

"You go ahead and let the kids look, okay, hon?"

Jonah nodded and popped a kiss against her cheek.

She would miss those too.

He and the kids clambered out and crossed the road to join the throng of excited people. For a moment, she stood at her door and watched them. Hand-in-hand, happy. Oblivious. Would this image of them be the one she pictured on lonely nights from now on?

She sighed as she grabbed her backpack from the floorboard. Jonah hadn't noticed the bag she always carried seemed a bit heavier than usual. Slipping into the dense foliage behind her, Olivia took one last glance at her family, and then let the branches snap back into place and obscure her from everyone.

Tears flowed down her cheeks as she crested the hill just inside the forest's edge. She swiped them away. She'd done what had to be done in order to save them. That's all that mattered.

Six months. A hundred and ninety two point five days since Dave had walked away. Had chosen the greener grass and left Annalise Baker standing in the muddy backwash. There were still days she felt as if she was barely hanging on by a thread.

Like today.

Annalise sighed. The pen shook as she scrawled her name on the papers granting Dave his divorce. He'd get the house. She'd get their dog Millie. And they'd both move on.

Right.

So easy to say. Much harder to actually do.

But the last thing she could do for the man she thought she would spend the rest of her life with was grant his wish. She hadn't focused enough on her marriage when she'd had a chance to save it, and now it was over. He hadn't fought hard enough when he felt it slipping away, and now he had someone new.

Her phone jingled, and she jumped. She glanced at the caller ID and smiled. "Hey, Zach. What's up?"

"Just checking on you."

Thank the good Lord above for her best friend, or she wouldn't have survived the upheaval that seemed to be her life recently. "I'm okay."

"Signed the papers, didn't you?"

"Just now." He'd read her mind so many times, she'd grown used to it by now. Counted on it, even.

"Ready to come work for SMIF now?"

Their mutual team leader Kirk had kept her on as a consulter for the Smoky Mountain Investigative Force while she figured out where life was dragging her. She had a sneaking suspicion Zach kept Kirk's doubts about her full return to work at bay with daily whisperings and encouragement. "Might as well. Nothing else to do with my free time now."

Zach chuckled. "You make it sound as if you've been handed a death sentence."

She had been, hadn't she? Divorce wasn't something she'd wanted, asked for, or ever seen coming. It meant she'd failed at the most important thing in her life.

"You deserve so much better, Lise. This divorce may just turn out to be your freedom papers instead."

She snorted. "Right."

"Seriously." He sighed. "Want to see the new headquarters with me today?"

She glanced around at the empty house. She literally had no reason to stay. All of her things already awaited her in a chalet above Gatlinburg, with a beautiful view and a massive fireplace. She couldn't afford it, but something about the home called to her. "I'm on my way."

Leaving the papers on the kitchen counter for Dave, along with more than one tear smudge, she walked out of her used-to-be home and closed the door for the last time.

It didn't hurt as much as she thought it would.

On the front walk, she drew in a long, slow breath and blew it out, sending negative thoughts and clouded emotions along with it. Dwelling on what could have been would only distract her from what actually was.

Zach was waiting on her. A new job. A new life. A new purpose.

A new Annalise Raven Baker. Special Agent Baker, nonetheless.

Ugh. If she kept up the self-pep-talk, maybe, eventually, somehow, she would start to believe it. Maybe somehow she would cast those lying, guilt-tripping demons out. The ones who yelled at her innermost thoughts, "You weren't enough. He would have stayed, wouldn't have run to her, had you been enough."

Her cell phone rang again. "Hey, Zach."

"Where you at?"

"Seriously? We talked like five seconds ago."

"Just making sure you didn't get lost."

She rolled her eyes but couldn't help the smile that spread across her face. Leave it to Zach to make her grin at a time like this. When her former world was falling to a giant pile of ashes—again—behind her, he had her looking toward the future. "Right. Look, I'm headed up now."

"No more standing on your ex's sidewalk reminiscing, okay?"

She sighed. "Fine, I give. You caught me."

"Life will be good again. You'll see."

She bit her lip. "How do you kn—" She caught herself. Of course he knew. He'd lived through his parent's divorce.

"Just hurry up, slow poke. We need to run through your testimony one more time before tomorrow too."

A stone plopped into her stomach, pulling her even lower. "Don't remind me."

"Get used to it, Special Agent. Part of the job description."

She rolled her eyes. "I know, I know."

"Jimmy Vern Buchanan needs to be locked away—as long as humanly possible. You're ready to seal that coffin, aren't you?"

Cody Moss's face flashed through her mind's eye. He hadn't deserved to be kidnapped, starved nearly to death, his mother beaten, his friends threatened—she didn't need to go on. The list was longer than her new book of regrets. "Yes."

"There's my girl."

"Listen, best friend, you think you know me so well…"

Zach's laughter shot through the phone.

She pulled it away from her ear and chuckled. Who was she kidding? He did know her that well. Creepy well sometimes. "I'll be there in forty-five minutes."

"You officially moved out in?"

"Out in?"

"Yeah, out of that jerk's house and into your own place."

She winced. Jerk? She wouldn't call Dave a jerk. He was sweet, handsome, considerate…and an adulterer. Jerk it was. "Yep. Got the very last things just now. Millie loves the new place, especially the bird feeder on the side deck." Annalise clenched her fist a bit tighter around her mother's locket. She'd almost forgotten it, hanging on the mirror above the antique dresser she and Dave had picked out. It seemed so long ago now. A lifetime had passed in just the last six months.

She would never be the same woman.

Was that a good thing or a bad one?

"Lise, get out of your own head."

"Hmm?"

"Stop. Thinking."

"Hard to do."

He chuckled. "For you, yes. For me, not so much."

"That is the most honest thing you've said in a while."

"Just get down here. I have new cross-examination questions for you. After I show you the headquarters. Fully functional kitchen. Might be my favorite part."

"Might be?"

"Yep. I like the grill on the patio too."

"Of course you do." It involved food. "I can't talk and drive."

"As you wish." Click.

"Bye to you too, you big goofball." Her chuckle died in her throat. She didn't want to run through her testimony again. It was too hard to think clearly right now, with her broken heart sending shockwaves every five seconds to the rest of her body. Zach had far too much fun the day before pretending she was on the stand and ripping her apart, and she had no desire to repeat the torture.

If she pretended like court wasn't actually happening tomorrow, she could delay the piranhas eating her from the stomach out. Right?

Chapter Two

"You could live here, Zach."

His eyes lit up. "I know!"

"Did you actually design everything yourself?"

"Nope. Kirk read my mind."

"And how about the woman in your guys's midst? Any consideration at all for her desires?" Annalise actually liked the headquarters, with its high, open-beamed ceilings and rustic-cabin feeling, but she couldn't miss a chance to give him a hard time.

"Follow me, m'lady."

"Oh, well, when you say it like that, what choice do I have but to comply?" She grinned. Her first spontaneous smile in days felt good. Really good.

Zach held the back door open and let her pass.

Annalise stopped in her tracks and gasped.

"Your own private oasis, Lise. This, I did design myself."

Encircled by tall, fragrant hedges, a shaded fountain and an inviting bench waited for her. "It's beautiful."

"Count the feeders."

Five? "How many birds do we plan to attract here?"

"As many as you like. Kirk said you can even bring Millie if you want. She can hang out and be the office pet."

Annalise flew into his arms and squeezed his waist tight. "Thank you, Zach. Really."

"I knew you would need somewhere quiet and outdoorsy to be able to let that beautiful mind of yours think properly. Can't have our newest special agent having brain-block in the middle of a serious case, can we?"

She chuckled. "I suppose not." The weight of their confidence in her abilities settled onto her shoulders. What if she let the guys down? What if Dave's affair and the divorce had played such havoc with her thought processes that she was no longer suited for this line of work? Mental clarity hadn't exactly been her strong suit lately.

"Stop thinking, Annalise."

"Ugh. I don't know how."

He kissed the top of her head and squeezed. "You'll figure it out. You're stronger than you know."

For a moment longer, she lingered in the safety of his arms. "You smell good today."

"What? I smell good every day."

She released him, and he dropped his arms. "Oh, yeah, especially after that hike into the mountains last year to get Buchanan's men."

He raised his hands in surrender. "Extenuating circumstances."

Her smile bloomed even bigger. "Come on. Let's go practice. If we must…"

"We must. You are still nervous as a cat in a room full of rocking chairs."

"Long-tailed cat, Zach. Long-tailed."

"Short tails hurt gettin' rocked on too."

Oh, for Pete's sake. She would have thought by now she could follow his lines of thoughts a little better.

Annalise grimaced. Again. He was tempted to point it out. Again. But he refrained. He'd been mock questioning her for an hour. If he pushed much harder, she'd break and forget everything they'd practiced when she made it to court tomorrow.

The office phone rang, and Zach heard Kirk's muffled voice answer in the next office. A few moments later, he poked his head in the doorway. "Got a call. Come on."

He glanced at Annalise. Her face drained of color. What was that about? She was tailor-made for this job. He sighed. Dave had robbed her of her confidence. The last six months had been torture watching her blame herself for the demise of their marriage. Maybe a new case was exactly what she needed right about now.

"I made you a gear bag."

Her gaze snapped to his. "You did? That was thoughtful of you."

"That's me." He inflated his chest. "Mr. Thoughtful." More like Mr. Concerned. And a hint of some other things he'd been managing to stuff down for months now.

Zach grabbed shotgun, after tucking Annalise into the rear passenger seat and closing her door. She shot him a look that said, "You're babying me too much, bud." Guilty. He knew he was. He'd have to back off a touch and let the little birdie try out her broken wings.

"Quit thinking, Zach."

He grinned. "Touché."

Kirk cast him a sideways glance with a raised-eyebrow.

Zach shook his head. "What's the call?"

"Lost woman in Cades Cove."

"When did she disappear?"

"Coupla hours ago."

"Why did they just now call?" Annalise spoke up from the rear.

"Thought surely they'd find her. A couple here with their two children. Stopped to look at a black bear up a tree, and when the husband turned around the wife was gone. No trace of her whatsoever."

"Wow."

Zach's heart pounded to life. How on earth had no one seen the woman? How had they been looking for her for two hours and found no leads? Why would she vanish, just like that? He shivered. Though he couldn't picture the details of his father's face anymore, the feelings were as vivid as when he'd received the news as a teenager.

Your father left, Zachary. His mother had been so calm giving him the news. Had it not been for the single tear glistening in the corner of each eye, he wouldn't have known she cared at all.

"Zach?" Annalise tapped him on the shoulder.

"Huh?"

"Did you put Sawyer water filters in the pack?"

"Oh, um, yeah."

She chuckled. "Ironic."

What?

"The Buchanan case. That's what they always carried."

"Right."

She leaned forward and whispered in his ear. "You okay?"

A chill fluttered over him as her breath brushed against his neck. He leaned toward the window and cleared his throat. "Yeah, I'm fine."

He wasn't fine. She could tell. But, with Kirk five inches away, now was the not the time to question him. Was he just still worried about her? If so, he'd have to get over it. She was the one who would be fine. Till she had to go home alone, to a dark cabin…

She shook her head. She'd have plenty of time to worry about that later.

"You have court tomorrow. Right, Annalise?"

Her gaze refocused on Kirk's profile. "Yes, sir."

"I hope you get some sleep tonight. No telling how long we'll be out."

She choked back a laugh. Sleep? Not likely, even if she was home.

The rest of the trip, they rode in silence. Each lost in their own thoughts? Apprehensions? Hopes? She certainly was.

Maybe she needed a new hobby. Something to occupy her evenings by the fire as the last of the spring chill ebbed away. Crocheting, possibly. Or whittling. Right, like she could picture herself whittling. Though it would fit her new cabin-living life.

"What's so funny?" Zach grinned over his shoulder at her.

Oops. She hadn't meant to actually laugh aloud. "Nothing. Trying to decide if whittling might suit me."

Zach's laughter filled the space.

"You know maybe for that reaction, I just might give it a try."

His laugh intensified, until Kirk and she couldn't help but join in.

Kirk made his way slowly around the relatively uncluttered Cades Cove loop. Around a bend, flashing lights pulled off the side marked the obvious location of the woman's disappearance. Park rangers, several with hats in their hands, waited, their anxiety evident in the way they carried their stiff shoulders and in the grim lines of their mouths.

As they exited the vehicle, one broke from the group and approached Kirk. "I'm Blu."

Annalise smiled. He certainly was, with those big, gorgeous eyes like a summer sky. His flawless coffee-creamer skin and curly light brown hair. Oh, my.

Zach turned to her. "You coming?"

She hadn't realized she had stopped dead in her tracks. "Yep." As soon as she could tear her gaze from handsome Ranger Blu.

Zach followed her gaze and frowned.

A blush flowed into her cheeks. She wanted to argue with the look on Zach's face. The one that made her feel guilty for being too-newly single to look at a man that way. But he was probably right. It was much too soon.

They joined the in-progress update Ranger Blu was giving to the circle of officials. "Olivia Beck, age thirty-nine, missing since approximately ten this morning. We have moved all available witnesses to the amphitheater behind the general store at the beginning of the loop. I've been informed the Smoky Mountain Investigative Force is here, and they will be covering interviews. The rest of us, we will fan out and begin a grid search."

Annalise leaned close to Zach. "What have they been doing for the last two hours?"

"Special Agent Baker?" Blu pinned her with a boring gaze.

"Yes?"

"You have a question to share with the rest of us?"

Was this the academy again? She cleared her throat. "Yes, actually. I was just wondering what steps you have already taken."

He stared her through for a moment before answering. "We've swept the periphery, as is protocol, looking for any trace of Mrs. Beck. We have questioned her husband and both children." He paused. "They are understandably upset, but, unfortunately, are as clueless as we are."

Clueless? She frowned. It had only been two hours. Wasn't it much too early to admit such a level of defeat? Her original impression of Blu fell from its pedestal a few notches.

Kirk drove them back out of the loop to the area behind the general store, where they were to begin organizing and interviewing the potential witnesses. Annalise hadn't expected there to be so many.

Zach sighed. "Shoulda known, I suspect. Seems like everybody in the loop ends up at the black bears at the same time."

"Yeah, I suppose. Means we have more potential leads, though, right?"

"Right," Kirk said. "Let's split them up in three groups and dive in."

Annalise's first witness was a couple from Ohio, vacationing in Gatlinburg. "Where were you when our missing person disappeared?"

"In the crowd," the elder man said.

"And where was that?"

"At the base of the tree. We honestly didn't see a thing, officer." A blush climbed his cheeks.

"We were watching the bear. Fascinating creatures, aren't they?" The wife seemed to have no embarrassment whatsoever at having been among the crowd much too close to the bear.

"You realize that there is a 300-yard radius recommended for animal viewing, right?"

They both nodded.

"We just got so excited. Never seen a black bear in person before." The wife smiled sheepishly.

"Did you see the missing woman in the crowd?" Annalise looked to each in turn. Both of them shook their head.

"Okay, thank you. Please write your contact information on this notepad, just in case we have follow-up questions."

The story was much the same from each of the twenty-two witnesses Annalise interviewed. All eyes had been on the bear, not the crowd, nor who was missing from it. She glanced across the picnic shelter to where Zach stood with the few witnesses he had left. By the crease in his brow, she suspected he was getting the same answers.

Kirk had disappeared at least half an hour before.

Annalise refocused on the last set of people approaching her. "I'm Special Agent Baker. How are you today?"

"What a shame! We came to enjoy this beautiful East Tennessee spring weather and now some horrible crime has happened." The middle-aged woman twisted her hands together.

Annalise took a deep breath and blew it out slowly. "We are not certain yet what happened, ma'am. If you will refrain from jumping to conclusions, we would appreciate it. Did you see anything that could be of help, ma'am?"

"No, but Gerald did." She pointed at her husband, standing a bit behind and to the left.

Annalise's heart skipped a beat. "Sir, can you describe exactly what you saw?"

"Charlene jumped out of the truck and ran over to the tree. I took a moment to put in a new dip of Copenhagen. As I got out of the truck, I saw a woman with a camera and a backpack headed into the woods in the opposite direction."

Annalise squeezed the pen in her hand tighter. This was legitimately helpful information. "Can you describe the woman?"

"She was short, maybe about five-five, long light brown hair. Wearing blue jeans, a dark hoodie sweatshirt, a dark green backpack, and a ball cap."

Wow. This guy was observant. She quirked an eyebrow.

"I was a police officer."

Ah. Not just helpful, but reliable information too. "This is great. Thank you."

"I can take you back to the exact spot she went into the woods."

Charlene patted her husband's arm and smiled up at him, the glimmer in her eyes evidence of her pride. "I'll wait here, dear. Might have me some of that famous soft-serve ice cream."

Gerald pecked her on the cheek. "Ready, Special Agent?"

Annalise hadn't even had time to tuck her pen and notepad away. "Ready. Let me radio my boss and let him know."

She motioned Zach to a quiet corner and filled him in, then she radioed Kirk and asked him to meet them at the Jeep. It was the only viable lead they had. There was no time to waste.

Chapter Three

Zach's stomach burned. Annalise had to stop looking at Blu that way. Period. And Blu definitely, beyond the shadow of a doubt, needed to cease, immediately, staring at her when she wasn't looking. With a bear-like mental growl, he forced his attention back to Gerald and Kirk's conversation.

Eight officers were out in the dense forest somewhere, combing the ground for any signs of Mrs. Beck. They hadn't started in the right place, if Gerald remembered the details as clearly as he claimed.

"She went between these low hemlock branches." Gerald pointed to a place fifty yards from where the search had begun. "I thought maybe she needed to sneak away and find a private tree, if you know what I mean."

Kirk nodded.

"But once I went to join Charlene, I plumb forgot about it. Until you all showed up and corralled everyone from the loop."

"You're sure?" Kirk pressed.

"Positive. She separated them, paused a moment, and then vanished. The woods are so thick right now, you could hide an elephant out there and no one would know."

The older man was right. They were fighting an uphill battle against forces of nature much stronger than they. But if they repositioned and started over, maybe they would find something—anything—to point them in the right direction.

Blu radioed the group of park rangers and asked that they return to ground zero.

"Let's take a peek, Annalise."

"Okay."

"Lead the way."

Zach followed Annalise through the foliage. It took less than thirty seconds to realize there were too many needles and leaves coating the ground for any prints. Unless Mrs. Beck dropped something, snagged a piece of fabric on a thorn, or they ran into her, there would be no way to know which way she'd gone.

"Why do you think she came this way, when everyone else went that way?" Annalise pointed behind them.

"Dunno. Maybe she saw another bear?"

"Maybe."

"Maybe she did need a 'private tree' like Gerald said."

"I guess that's always possible. It would've been the perfect time, I suppose, with everyone else distracted."

Kirk's call sailed into the forest, bidding them back to the waiting vehicles.

"This is going to be one of those cases where you never get answers." Zach mumbled it, not even completely realizing he'd said it aloud until Annalise stopped in front of him and turned.

"We didn't think we'd find Cody Moss either. Did we?"

He didn't. She'd managed to hang onto an immense amount of hope considering the circumstances. "You're right. I'm sorry."

"What's eating you today?"

How could he explain the emotions churning within him? He knew he could trust her with anything, it wasn't that. But if he gave voice to their annoying little somersaults, jabs, and snickers, he'd awaken the same old hurts. The same ones he'd tried so hard to ignore. So hard to pretend he'd dealt with. Later. "Speaking of eating, I'm hungry."

Annalise rolled her eyes.

He could tell by the way she studied him a moment more that he hadn't pacified her for long.

Back at the truck, Kirk waited in the driver's seat. "We need to go speak to Mr. Beck."

"Where is he?" Annalise asked as she let herself into the back seat.

"Home. Blu let him and the kids go. Said it would be less stressful for the children."

Oh, wasn't Mr. Blu just the best? Never mind the fact the most critical witnesses had left the scene.

But an hour and a half later, when Zach saw the pained expressions on the children's faces, some of his critical gusto melted away. These poor kids were scared and hurting. As much as he hated to admit it, Blu had probably been right in allowing their father to take them home.

"Mr. Beck," Kirk began almost as soon as they entered the foyer, "can you tell us anything at all that might be helpful?"

"No. I have run it over and over in my mind." Mr. Beck sank into a chair. "I have no idea what happened. One moment Olivia was there. The next she wasn't. It's like she just...vanished. Into thin air."

People kept using that word. No one simply vanished. They were forced to leave or they chose to leave. Simple as that. His father had chosen. End of story. Close the book. And burn it.

"What brought you to the Cove today?"

Annalise hovered in a dimly lit corner, watching the man's reaction.

She was better at analyzing people than Zach, and he was pretty good. He was so glad she'd joined their team.

"Olivia has been dreaming of the 'perfect shot' of a black bear for years. We go at least once every fall and every spring to try."

"Shot?" Kirk's pen stopped midair.

"She's an amateur photographer. Stunning work. Our bedroom is lined with her favorite ones. Want to see?"

Kirk shook his head. "Not necessary."

"I'd like to see," Annalise spoke up.

"Andi, can you take Agent Baker to Mommy and Daddy's room?"

The young girl nodded, swiping tears from her cheeks as she turned. Her brother followed silently.

"This has been a nightmare." Mr. Beck's voice dropped to a whisper. "I can't believe it's real. She has to be there...somewhere. Just beyond where you've looked. Doesn't she?"

"We certainly won't give up searching, Mr. Beck."

Zach crossed his arms over his chest and leaned into the doorframe. As far as he could tell, Mr. Beck was distraught. Genuinely concerned without malicious undertones that made him a suspect in the disappearance. For the children's sake, he hoped it stayed that way.

"Which is your favorite, Andi?" Annalise squatted next to the thin girl.

She raised a skinny arm and pointed at a dark-matted photo of a monarch butterfly perched delicately on a rhododendron.

"Oh, that is beautiful. They all are." Annalise drew a deep breath. "Your Mommy is very talented."

Andi nodded.

Behind her, Annalise heard Drew sigh.

"That one's my favorite." His quiet voice filled the space between Annalise and Andi.

Annalise turned to gaze at the one he indicated. "That one is very lovely. I especially like how the light makes the water reflect the sunset almost like a perfect mirror."

"Are you gonna find our Mommy?" Andi stuck her hand in Annalise's and squeezed.

Annalise squeezed back, her heart constricting in her chest to the point of near-stopping. She swallowed hard and whispered, "I'm going to try my best."

Not every case ends like this one, Annalise. Zach's pessimism rang so loudly in her mind she wanted to cover her ears.

Maybe just one more miracle-ending case, Lord? These kids need their mom.

Drew and Andi retreated softly from the room.

She quickly riffled through the nightstand drawers, flicked open and closed the medicine cabinet, and made one more thorough inspection of the photographs. When she returned to the living room, Kirk and Zach held a quiet conversation near the fireplace. Mr. Beck was nowhere to be seen.

"There are medicines for Jonah Beck in the bathroom, but there are none for Olivia. Either she was in perfect health or she took them with her."

"Good work, Annalise." Kirk made a note in his pad.

"She's a talented photographer. I think that part of the story rings true, for what it's worth."

Kirk and Zach nodded.

"Let's get back out there. Those guys need our help." Zach grinned.

"I need to drive separately this trip. Just in case. Can't miss court in the morning."

"Oh, right. That's fine, Annalise. I'll drop you back at the station, and then I will feed this monster something before we go back into the loop."

Zach pouted while Annalise and Kirk chuckled.

He was like Dr. Jekyll and Mr. Hyde. Thankfully, even on an empty stomach, Mr. Hyde wasn't so intolerable.

Back in her own vehicle, aimed for Cades Cove for the second time that day, Annalise dialed her mom.

"Hello, daughter!"

"Hello, mother!"

"How are you, my dear?" Rynata Baker always greeted her only child in the same manner.

It used to drive Annalise mad, but now she treasured the sound of her mother's voice, floating an entire continent across satellite signals. Today, even more. How long had it been since she'd checked in just because? Too long, for sure. "I'm fine, Mom. How are you and Dad?"

"Oh, just dandy."

Though her parents had moved to California somewhere along the third or fourth year of her marriage to Dave, her mother would never kick the Southern twang and country dialect. Annalise hoped not, anyway. "What's new?"

"Not much. Your dad bought another motorcycle. He says if he can get this one running 'right,' we're coming cross-country to see you."

Annalise choked on her Sprite. "By motorcycle?"

"You know your father. Big ideas."

"Yeah."

"Big dreams, Annalise. Never hurts to have 'em."

They'd always told her the same thing, as far back as she could remember. She used to believe it. Maybe not so much anymore since Dave chose *her*.

"You okay, baby girl?"

"Signed the papers earlier today. And now we have a missing tourist."

Her mom's loud sighed echoed through the speaker. "Oh, sweetie, I'm so sorry. I wish we'd known then what we know now about the pond scum jerk."

Ouch. Was it normal to still love your ex? The one who'd clearly moved on with his mistress and forgotten all about you in less time than it took to plan the beautiful, perfect-day wedding that spring day seven years ago? The wedding where that she-devil mistress was nowhere in sight—either physical or premonitionally.

"I just wanted to say I love you, Mom. I'm about to be out of cell service again."

"Be careful, baby girl. We love you too." Her mom kissed the air. "Oh, and I hope you find the tourist."

"Thanks. Me too. See you soon?"

"I'll be the one with helmet hair and unable to walk after riding five bazillion miles on the back of your father's bike." She laughed. "But I'll also be the one smiling."

Annalise envied her parents's relationship. She thought she'd found the same kind of forever with Dave. Apparently, great investigator that she was, she'd misread him all along. A tear slipped down her cheek. She swiped it away and made sure the person in the car next to her hadn't seen. Why? She wasn't sure. But it seemed vitally important no one spot her weakness.

Chapter Four

What on earth could Blu be saying that was so blame funny? And when had Annalise last laughed like that? His mental bear awoke and roared.

"You okay over there?" Kirk cocked his head and glanced at him from the driver's seat.

"Fine."

"'Cause you just growled."

Oops. Apparently, the inner bear controlled the outer goofball.

"It wouldn't have anything to do with that, would it?" Kirk pointed at Annalise standing with Blu several yards away.

The instantaneous burn of his cheeks gave him away. "We have work to do. Come on."

Kirk thrust the Jeep in park and hopped out.

Zach took a deep breath. What was going on with him? Annalise was his best friend. He wanted her to be happy. Right?

He wanted her to be protected more, though.

That was all this heat in his belly and scalding in his veins meant. He worried about her with anyone new. It was too soon.

"Hey, Zach. What took you guys so long?" Annalise beamed a radiant smile on him.

"Um, dinner?"

She rolled her eyes. "Of course."

He sighed with relief when Blu moved on to another group. "What's happening?"

"We are starting over. Entering the woods with fresh supplies where Gerald pointed out. The plan is to send in teams of five in parallel-to-the-road directions."

He nodded. That sort of made sense. "What if she went straight in?"

"No way to know, but we've got to start somewhere. The dogs are on their way and two mounted rangers. If we don't find her by nightfall," Annalise glanced at the sky, "we will camp in separate groups and resume in the morning. Well, you will. Not me."

"You want me to come with you?" Please let her say yes.

Man, when had he gotten so needy?

"Nah. I mean, I do, but I want you to find Mrs. Beck even more."

At least she did want him. Probably not as much as he wanted her.

Whoa.

The emotionally charged images that flooded his brain were suddenly not so platonic. He cleared his head and stepped out into a long stride. Anything it took to put some distance between them.

"Zach, wait!"

"We're losing daylight." He snapped more than he should have. When he glanced at her, his tone shone in the frown on her face. "Sorry," he whispered. What was wrong with him?

Lord, a little guidance here? Please. I don't mean to feel this way. I don't even really know how I feel. All I know is that something's wrong. Show me how to fix it, please.

Annalise's warm hand squeezing his shoulder snapped him out of his prayer. "You okay?"

"Fine." He sighed. "Thanks. I'll be fine."

"You're on my team, Zach. Hope you like the snacks I packed for you."

"Snacks?" Her smile made him chuckle. "You're like an overgrown teenager."

"Yep. Ain't denying that one. Speaking of teenagers, how is Paul?"

"I talked to Captain Brooks day before last. Said that 'the boy is settlin' in just fine.' "

"Your imitation is spot-on."

"I'll take that as a compliment. I think." She punched his shoulder. "Let's go."

He and Annalise joined their other three team members and stepped into the forest. If this worked, it would be a wonder. A miracle, like finding Cody alive half a year ago. Hikers that went into the Smokies off-trail were rarely found alive. Bears, cliffs, starvation…so many things could go wrong.

"How much outdoor experience did Mrs. Beck have?"

Annalise didn't turn at his question, but her voice carried over her shoulder in the otherwise quiet forest. "Her husband said they hiked frequently, but always on trails. He didn't think his wife had ever been backcountry before."

Not good. What was that woman's name who disappeared off the AT in Maine? He couldn't remember. They'd searched for her for months and finally had to give up when winter set in. It took something like six years to find her body. And then, it was on accident.

If it wasn't for the fact there was a missing woman somewhere ahead—or behind or left or right. He sighed. Only God knew for certain where Mrs. Beck was—it would be a beautiful day for hiking. Warm in the sunshine but cool under the canopy of hemlocks, oaks, and maples.

A few hundred feet into the forest, they spread into a line and pressed ahead slowly like soldiers on a front. Instead of eyes on the horizon though, their gazes were pinned to the ground. Any trace of a footprint or wrapper or broken twig would be flagged and GPS marked.

Was his father a hiker? Did he like being outside as much as Zach did?

Zach ground to a halt. How many years and years had it been since he'd had a thought like that?

"Find something?" Annalise called from a knoll nearby.

He shook his head. Nothing pertaining to Olivia Beck. Maybe something he'd rather leave behind. He resumed his slow pace.

In the distance, a woman shouted. Almost as one, the entire team froze. They were probably all thinking the same thing as he. Was that her? Was she calling for help? He held his breath and waited for a second cry. Their collective sigh filtered through the trees when five minutes of silence passed.

"Could anyone tell which direction that originated?" Kirk shouted.

In turn, they each answered no.

What if that was their one chance? Their one shot at locating the missing wife and mother.

It'd be just fantastic if Annalise's first official case with SMIF ended in tragedy. Or worse, open ends that could never be solved. He could hear her argument already. "I'm not a kid, Zach." No, she certainly wasn't. Not anymore. Why did he insist on handling her with kid gloves then?

Again, they moved forward as one multi-limbed unit. No one whispered or hollered jokingly back and forth this time. Had the reality of the challenge ahead settled heavily on them like it had Zach? A woman whom three people loved very much was out there surrounded by so many unknowns it felt as if there weren't any knowns at all.

Just like his dad.

Gone without a trace before Zach was man enough to not need a man's influence. Gone before Zach could tell him how much he loved him, and then, over the years, how much he hated him. For what he did to his mother. For what he did to him. For just not being there at all.

Annalise cast another sidelong glance toward Zach. What in the world was going on with him? She hadn't seen that deep furrow in his brow in…well, she couldn't remember the last time. And that snappy tone he kept lobbing her way. When had he ever spoken to her in that voice? When they were teenagers? Possibly. When his dad—

Annalise sucked in a breath. When Zach's dad left. That's the last time he'd been so touchy that he was off-limits. Was that it?

She opened her mouth to yell her question to him. There were too many onlookers. If she thought he was agitated now, wait until she embarrassed him in front of Kirk and the others. She clamped her mouth shut and made a mental note to ask him as soon as they were alone.

The evening sun pierced the canopy in long shafts. It would be fully dark in two hours, and their search would be slowed down even more. But, at least Olivia would probably be stopping too. If she wasn't already forced to stop by injury or... Annalise forced her focus on the ground. No sense borrowing trouble.

Three hours and two slow, heart-in-her-throat miles later, with the glow of the campfire and the men's voices keeping the quiet forest companionable, Annalise pulled Olivia Beck's file from her backpack and began studying the woman's life.

Short, light brown hair in a stylish pixie cut framed a slender face. Paired with Olivia's petite nose and bright green eyes, gorgeous wasn't an overstatement.

Olivia held a master's degree in elementary education and for the last five years had taught at Coalfield Elementary. Educated locally at The University of Tennessee. She'd probably been on campus at the same time as Annalise. They may have passed each other in the halls or on the sidewalks. If only Annalise had known then what she knew now.

Annalise frowned. If she had known what she knew now, what would she have done? Run up to the woman, shaken her shoulders, and said, "Never go off the side of the Cades Cove loop trail and get lost in the woods." Right. That made so much sense.

No criminal history. Not even as much as a parking violation.

Married to Jonah Beck in 2011.

Same year as she and Dave. Apparently Jonah was better at keeping his marriage vows than Dave.

Two kids, Andi and Drew, ages five and four. Soccer, minivan, house in a quiet neighborhood, two dogs, one horse. Olivia checked off all the "perfect life" boxes.

Annalise returned to the photograph, something niggling the recesses of her mind. The eyes. There was something about them that seemed so familiar. Could it simply be that they'd gone to school together? That they may have shared a class at some point?

Maybe. But that was eons ago. There was something else there. If she could just remember it.

"Don't you think you'd better head back, Annalise?"

Zach's quiet voice close to her shoulder made her jump. "Yeah, probably." She turned to face him. "This was an accident, right?"

"What makes you ask?"

"She had the perfect life. No one in their right mind would leave it. It has to be an accident."

"You had the perfect life too, Annalise. From the outside looking in, I mean."

He had a good point. "Did you believe Jonah was being forthcoming with us?"

He tilted his head and glanced away for a moment. "Yeah. I think so. He seemed genuinely distraught, didn't he?"

She nodded. He was right. Besides, it would've been impossible for Jonah to sneak away from the crowd and do something to Olivia. She stretched the tension from her shoulders. "I had better go. Big day tomorrow." Big day that she dreaded was more accurate.

"Want me to hike back with you?"

"Nah, I'll be fine."

"I know you will. But I don't mind."

She put her hand on his shoulder and smiled. "Thanks. Stay here. Get some rest. I'll be back after court."

"Be safe. I'd like to see your beautiful face again. You know, not mauled by a bear."

She chuckled. "That would be quite inconvenient for my face."

"Agreed." He dipped his chin. "And for me."

"Oh, please!" She punched his arm. "You'd be glad to be rid of this pest."

He grinned. "Right."

She returned his grin, but something different about the look on his face made her pause. Zach was acting weird. Were the sparks igniting his gaze just reflections of the firelight?

Chapter Five

Annalise's fitful sleep made her more tired than if she'd stayed up all night. Her hands shook as she pulled on each of the outfits she'd thought might work. The first one was too low-cut. The second, too tight. Too loose. Too short. Too bright. Finally, twenty minutes after she intended to leave, she walked out the front door and headed for the court room. In the first outfit, with a different undershirt.

It was going to be a long day.

Court rooms in real life never looked like the fancy-smancy ones on television. Annalise was relieved. There was too much pressure in those grand cinematic rooms. At least in real-life, the room's expectation of its witnesses was far less. Show up, be honest.

She could do that.

In the hallway, she ran into Cody and Celine Moss. Cody's father, Brian, and his family waved to her from farther down the plain-walled area. "It is so good to see you guys." She embraced each in turn. "How are you feeling, Cody?"

"I'm better, ma'am."

"I'm so glad. Celine? All healed up?" The man they were there to see trialed today had inflicted some nasty damage on this strong woman.

"I can tell when it's going to rain now, but other than that, I'm better." Celine wrapped an arm around her son's shoulders. "As long as my boy's home, I can't complain."

Annalise smiled, but it quickly fell. "Are y'all ready for today?" They were both to be called as witnesses too.

Celine and Cody nodded.

They didn't seem to have a single jitter. Resolute was a good word.

For them.

A quaking, unsure mess was more accurate for her. It was ridiculous. She was a professional, and she had testified before. The only difference now was all the awful things Dave had said. How could one man's ugly comments affect her so severely?

She leaned against the wall next to them and crossed her arms over her chest. Was Jimmy Vern already in there? With that smug look on his face and total lack of remorse. Two days after his full confession, he'd retracted his statement, claiming he was under duress and tricked into talking without a lawyer. Figured. The man would say or do anything to avoid responsibility for his own actions.

A bailiff poked his head out the door. "Quiet in the hallways. Trial begins in five minutes."

Annalise turned her cell phone off. *Lord, help Zach and the others this morning.* She wished she was there instead. Ugh. She wished she was anywhere other than here.

Another courtroom, in another city, in another lifetime, materialized in her memory. She'd testified against a powerful politician then, not a backwoods, moonshine-making, mountain man. Both men flooded their respective markets with illegal products harmful to the community.

Memphis hadn't ended so well for Annalise though.

What if this time was the same?

She chuckled. She didn't own a house to be burned down right now. And her marriage had ended on the tail end of the Jimmy Vern Buchanan case, so hadn't things already gone poorly for her? What more did she have to lose?

Silence blanketed the hallway so thick only the sound of the air moving through the overhead ducts broke it. What was happening on the other side of those doors? How long would they sit, and wait, and pray for justice?

"Cody Moss, you may enter the courtroom." The same bailiff held the door for the teen.

Annalise patted his mother's hand and smiled.

"I wish I could go in there with him. At least his dad is. That's something anyway, right?"

"I'm sure Cody will be fine, Celine. He is one of the strongest boys I've ever met."

Celine returned Annalise's hand squeeze. "You're right. He's stronger than I am."

"Me too."

Celine sighed and stared into Annalise's eyes until Annalise squirmed. "I am so sorry about your divorce. Are you okay?"

Ah, the small town grapevine remained intact. "Thank you. I'm fine." Lying to the sweet woman burned. But Annalise couldn't afford to go into details right now. Not when—

The court room door flew open, and Cody stormed out.

"What in the world?" Celine took off after him.

Escorted by two armed guards, Jimmy Vern shuffled through the door next. He paused, lifted his shackled hands in mock salute, and smiled at Annalise.

Her stomach turned. The nerve!

Jimmy Vern scooted down the hallway as if he were on a slightly-hampered-by-the-leg-chains stroll through the park.

What was happening? Annalise waited a few moments and then peeked into the empty courtroom. Where had the lawyers and the bailiff and the judge gone?

Was she asleep? She had to be. There was no other explanation.

"What's going on?"

Annalise spun to find Captain Brooks lingering behind her with Paul. "Hey, guys." She hugged them both. "I have no idea. Court started and then stopped, like that." She snapped. "You don't think they—"

Milt Brooks, her former captain from Norris Police Department, held up his hand. "I'll find out. Don't jump to conclusions just yet." Captain Brooks disappeared into an office down the hall.

"How are you doing, Paul?"

The teen dipped his chin. "I'm good, Ms. Baker." He blushed.

"Things going well in your new home?"

Paul nodded.

"I'm so glad."

"Me too."

She almost didn't hear the last two words, whispered though they were as he turned away.

Captain Brooks returned a moment later. "Plea bargain."

"What!" Annalise's heart thundered to life. "How? What? Who?"

"I don't know, Annalise. Won't tell me a thing."

"What are the terms?"

"All they said was Buchanan entered a guilty plea and agreed to give information in exchange for not getting the death penalty."

If they'd offered him something like that, when they had so much evidence against the man, Jimmy Vern must know some seriously important secrets.

"But…but…" Annalise wasn't sure what argument she wanted to utter, but she certainly wanted to protest.

Zach glanced at his watch again. Was Annalise in the courtroom yet? Being in the mountains with no cell service really stunk on a day like this. If he could just shoot her a quick text, he would feel so much better.

Their morning campfire lay several miles behind. The search and rescue dogs wandered several miles ahead. And he and the other searchers carefully scoured the area between. But with each forward step, the hope of finding Olivia Beck grew dimmer. There was no sign of foul play. No bear attack. No random cliff with a body at the bottom. There was no sign at all.

The sun-and-shadow mottled ground stretched before them like a treasure map none of them had the legend to. If the clumps of squishy moss could speak, they could tell which direction her footprints pointed. If the dry leaves were able, they could lead the way on the next breeze. If only the trees were markers, with branch hands that could point them in the right direction.

"I've got something!" The call came from someone just out of sight and to the north.

Zach froze in his tracks. What kind of something? Could this be an actual clue or just another empty lead? His heart skipped as he placed a large log to mark his spot and turned to join the others.

Kirk stooped over a piece of garbage. "Granola bar wrapper."

"Did the husband say whether or not he thought Mrs. Beck had provisions with her?" Zach looked at each of the eight men and women in turn.

They shook their heads.

"Yeah, he didn't mention that to us either." Zach's hopes extinguished.

Kirk slipped the wrapper into a clear evidence bag and tucked it into his backpack. "Everyone take a quick break. I'll radio the dog handlers and see if they've gotten anything."

He stepped a few feet away, and his radio crackled to life. "Anything, guys?"

"Negative," the first team responded.

"Nothing over here either," the second replied quickly.

Zach was starting to believe alien abductions might be an actual thing.

Chapter Six

Her blood still boiling, Annalise answered the unknown caller through her SUV's Bluetooth. "Hello?"

"Annalise, it's Zach."

"Hey, where are you?"

"Ranger station at Cades Cove. We stopped the ground search for today. There is literally not one single trace of Mrs. Beck. Not by the mounted team, the dogs, or us on foot. Nothing. Kirk wants to know if you can go back to the Beck's home and see if there is anything else you can uncover there."

"Okay." Her heart sank a little lower than it already was.

"How was court?"

"I don't want to talk about it."

"That bad, huh?"

"It's a long story." She snickered. "Actually, it's not."

"What happened?"

"He—"

"Yeah, I'm coming!"

Annalise heard Kirk's voice in the background and knew Zach's attention had been pulled away.

"Sorry, Annalise. I've got to run. We are coordinating an aerial search. I'll call you as soon as I can."

"Okay—"

The line went blank.

She turned around at the next stop light and aimed for the Beck home.

Mr. Beck's truck waited in the driveway. Andi and Drew's faces flitted into view through the lace-curtained front window when Annalise rang the doorbell. A few heavy footsteps later, the door swung open to reveal a tight-lipped Jonah.

"Mr. Beck, how are you today?" Ugh, that was a stupid question.

He tilted his head to the left.

"Sorry." She cleared her throat. "I need to ask you a few more questions and maybe take another look at your wife's things. Do you have a moment now?"

"It's really not a great time." Jonah glanced over his shoulder to where Drew waited in his soccer uniform.

"Would you mind if I just take a look around? I can lock up when I leave."

"Um…I don't know."

She flashed her most winning smile. "It won't take long, I promise."

He toyed with the keys in his hand "Okay, yeah. If it'll help, go ahead." He opened the door to allow her to enter. "Come on, kids."

"I don't want to go without Mommy," Drew whined as he walked out the door.

"I know, bud, but she will be home soon. She wouldn't want you to miss your game."

Annalise hoped she could help Jonah keep that particular promise. The odds were certainly stacked against them.

She slipped on some latex gloves and leafed through the stack of mail in the kitchen. A few magazines, four credit card offers, and the electric bill. Nothing significant there. Drew and Andi's artwork decorated the fridge and the walls in the breakfast nook. She checked the drawers, the cabinets, and the pantry. Everything seemed to be in its place. Well organized and tidy, as Annalise would expect it to be in a school teacher's home.

Why had Olivia walked into the forest? It made no sense.

In the hallway, Annalise stopped to scrutinize the wedding and baby photographs, drawn once again to Olivia's eyes. There was something so hauntingly familiar about them. Where did she know them from? She pressed her eyes closed and tried to empty her thoughts. A face—a ghost from her past—materialized.

But it couldn't be. Joanie Greene was dead.

Zach watched from the open helicopter door as the trees rushed by below. Kirk sat opposite him, his neck craned to look out the right side. They'd cover an area of about 1,200 square miles before dinner tonight. A twenty-mile radius of nothing but dense, old-growth forest canopy practically impenetrable to the naked eye, on the hope that Mrs. Beck was intuitive enough to leave them a clue.

He strained his eyes against the horizon, hoping to catch a glimpse of a trail of smoke. Against the backdrop of wispy clouds, it would have been nearly impossible.

Was it supposed to rain soon? He'd been so consumed with the search he hadn't even checked. And that was an oversight he wouldn't normally have made.

What was wrong with his focus? He shook his head and pressed the com button. "See anything, Kirk?"

"Nope. Nothing."

Hopefully, Annalise was having better luck. Or any luck at all.

It was impossible. Absolutely. Annalise stepped away from the photos in the hall, only to return. She covered up the lower half of Olivia Beck's face. The eyes resembled Joanie, without a doubt. Did Joanie have a sister?

Annalise squeezed her eyes shut and pictured the faces of Joanie's loved ones around her coffin. Mother and father, some aunts and uncles, church family. Her mind's eye was a bit fuzzy after all these years, but no, there was no sister. She shook her head. It was a coincidence, a doppelganger. Had to be.

In the office, she opened drawers and slid books from shelves only to find receipts, tax forms, and dust. Photo albums stuffed with Andi and Drew's lives filled the top tiers of the bookcase. Annalise thumbed through the first few. Births, birthday parties, Christmases, and other holidays pronounced a happy and well-adjusted family. Looks could be deceiving, but she just wasn't picking up on the vibe of secret-killer husband. Or desperate-to-get-out wife.

Annalise ran her fingertips over a photo of one of the children on their day of birth. Swaddled in a fuzzy-looking yellow blanket, rosy-faced, and tiny-sweet. Something deep inside ached. She always thought she didn't want children, but what if, maybe just a little, she did?

Her divorce stole more than just the dreams she held for her marriage. It stole her future. She'd spent the last six months adjusting to living alone for the first time since college. To only having Millie to talk to in the gray hours of dawn. To the idea that she would never grow old with the person she planned on.

She hadn't expected to feel grief over the lack of potential motherhood too. A wave of fear and sadness mingled with anger threatened to topple her. What was the rest of her lonely life going to be like?

Zach would remind her that she had her handsome, if always-hungry, best friend. And she would giggle and remember just how blessed she was to have him. But Zach was Zach. Would God ever bless her with a second love of her life? Or was divorce the penultimate sin, the kind from which she'd never recover enough to be in love again?

The doorbell sounding overhead startled her from her morose thoughts. She moved to inconspicuously peek through the curtain. Captain Brooks? What was he doing here?

She swung the door open and smiled. "Hi, Captain."

His jaw opened but no words came out.

"Do you need something? Do you know the Becks?"

He cleared his throat. "Um, no. No, I just wanted to swing by and see if you needed any help."

"Slow day in town?"

He chuckled. "Aren't they all?"

Norris was a modern-day Mayberry. "Good point. I could definitely use some help. I've got nothing. Zip. Zero. Nada."

"I'm happy to lend a hand."

"Thanks. What are you doing out this way?"

"Nothing much."

Halls wasn't a super long drive from Norris, but it wasn't exactly a swinging-by direction either. Strange. But the Captain's business was none of hers. "I've looked through the kitchen, bedroom, and bathroom. Was tackling the office now."

"Lead the way."

"I've done most of it already in here too. There is not one shred of evidence to suggest Mrs. Beck isn't lost like we suspect. But I can't help but feeling like I'm missing something."

"Why don't I finish up in here, and you can tackle the guest bedroom?" Captain Baker entered the office behind her.

"That would be great. Maybe a fresh set of eyes will be just what we need. Thanks."

The practically empty guest bedroom proved as fruitless as the rest of the house. Annalise sighed. There was nothing here. No insights. No magic beans of revelation about Mrs. Beck's location. She peeked back in the office. "Find anything?"

Captain Brooks spun. "Nope."

The closet door to his right had not been cracked open when she left. But of course he had checked it. Why was she questioning something so insignificant?

Captain Brooks slid his hand into his pocket.

Was a slip of paper hiding in his palm? "Sir?"

"Yes, Annalise?"

What was that? She wanted to ask but bit her tongue. This was Captain Brooks she was talking about. Trustworthy. Honest to a fault. Her friend. "Where's Paul today? I thought I might stop by and say hi to him."

Captain Brooks released a heavy sigh. "At home. Of course, you're welcome to drop by. Any time."

"I'm finished here, if you are."

"You were right. I don't see anything to point you in a foul-play direction."

Outside, she thanked him once more and watched as he drove away. She locked the front door and climbed into her SUV. The uneasy vibe she'd felt in the hallway staring at the photo of Mrs. Beck would not be smothered. Captain Brooks's odd behavior didn't help. Not one little bit. She needed to talk to Zach and bounce some ideas off him. Too bad he was in a helicopter somewhere over their search zone.

Chapter Seven

"Zach, I'm glad you called." Annalise curled her feet under her.

Millicent lifted her head from the couch next to Annalise as if to say, "I'm sleeping here, Mom. Do you have to move so much?"

Annalise patted the sweet beagle's soft head and smiled. "Find anything?"

"Not a thing."

The disappointment in his voice carried easily through the phone and matched up with hers.

"You?"

"No."

"What is it?"

"What is what?" Zach always could read her mind. Disturbingly so sometimes.

"Don't give me that, Annalise. You're not telling me something."

She sighed. "Captain Brooks stopped by the Beck's home today. He was acting weird."

Zach laughed. "Captain Brooks? Weird how?"

"I know, I know. Most dependable, rock-solid man I know. I'm tired and worried we won't figure this one out in time."

"Yeah, me too."

"I swear I saw him hide something in his pocket. And I can't figure out why he was at the house in the first place. How did he even know I was there?"

"This is Captain Milton Brooks we're talking about. If he was there, you can bet he had a good reason. And if he hid something, he needed to."

He was right. "I'm tired."

"Want me to come keep you company?"

Annalise scratched Millie's belly. "Nah. I think I'm going to turn in early tonight. Do you know what the plan is for tomorrow?"

"We are going to widen the search grid and try the dogs again at a different location farther north."

"Why north?"

"The advance team ran into a fairly steep mountain chain deep in the woods. The hope is that if Mrs. Beck made it that far she would turn toward the north."

"Or the south."

"That's the thing. No way to know for sure."

"Right." She twiddled a lock of hair between her fingers and sighed again, deeper. "I don't like this feeling of helplessness."

"No, I suspect you don't."

Something in his tone needled her. "What's that supposed to mean?"

"You like to be in control. It freaks you out when you aren't."

"Look, Zach, you're my best friend. But you don't know everything about me." He was wrong. She wasn't controlling. She liked to be in control. There was a difference.

"Fine. I surrender."

She could picture him with his hands in the air, palms out, grinning that annoying "I told you so" grin. "Good night, Zach."

"I'll pick you up at eight."

"I'll be ready for another long day." Of dead ends and a woman with the magic powers to disappear into thin air.

Annalise awoke thinking of Joanie Greene. Before her coffee had finished brewing, she had her laptop open Googling the newspaper clippings from Officer Greene's murder in late 2011.

The obituary boasted a head shot of Joanie in full uniform. Annalise held the photo of Mrs. Beck next to her computer. The resemblance was uncanny.

The same week that Senator Marcum's henchmen burned Annalise and Dave's house in Memphis, Joanie had died in a car accident across town. Suspicious circumstances with no proof. But Annalise had no doubt Senator Marcum had her killed.

In the courtroom, staring into the man's pompous face, he'd given Annalise a look similar to the one Buchanan gave her yesterday, instantly boiling her blood and forever convincing her of his guilt on more crimes than just the ones he'd been charged with.

Joanie had helped Annalise uncover the evidence that had led to Marcum's arrest. It was no coincidence that she was dead. None whatsoever.

Tears clouded Annalise's eyes. The fire was meant to take her out of the picture too. Senator Marcum's loose ends rarely survived.

Old feelings of inadequacy and frustration bubbled to the surface. For two years after her friend's death, Annalise had pursued every lead, thin as they all were, until she had no other choice but to surrender to failure. It wasn't long after that she'd requested her transfer to a quieter town.

There hadn't been much back then she could control either. And she hated it. With a passion. Being out of control terrified her. It was too close to spiraling, to crashing and burning and losing her marbles and failing at life.

She snorted. Kind of like the last six months. Ugh.

She'd snapped at Zach. He hadn't said she was controlling. He'd said exactly what she knew already. That spiraling out of control freaked her out. It wasn't so much that she needed to control others, but she needed to control herself...and everything that happened...she rolled her eyes and sighed. It was the same thing, wasn't it? She'd have to apologize to him in the morning.

And maybe go see Buchanan. She had questions for the dirtbag.

Zach knocked on the door a second time, then swung it open and peeked in. "Annalise?"

"In here!"

He strode through the entry hallway and into the open, high-ceilinged living room. He loved this cabin. If he'd found it first, Annalise might be visiting him. With its heavy pine beams and tall, stone fireplace, it was everything he'd ever pictured wanting. He handed her a cup of coffee and a blueberry muffin. "You okay?"

"Hmm? Yeah." She closed her laptop and smiled. "Just reminiscing."

Tears glistened in the corners of her eyes "About what, exactly?" Dave?

"Remember my partner, Joanie Greene?"

He nodded. Annalise had been devastated when Joanie died.

"Olivia Beck reminds me of her."

"Let me see."

Annalise opened the laptop once more and held up the photo of Mrs. Beck.

"Wow. That's crazy. Are you sure they aren't sisters?"

"Joanie never mentioned a sister, and there wasn't one at the funeral. Do you think maybe she had an estranged sister or cousin or something? Maybe that explains it?"

"They could be twins."

"I know."

"The noses and the brow shapes are different, but wow."

"I know."

He recognized the curious gleam in her eyes. Figuring out Olivia and Joanie's connection was going to quickly become Annalise's priority. "We'd better get moving."

"Yeah. Let me get my boots, and I'm ready."

"Did you see the story on the six o'clock news?"

"I caught the tail end of it. Any leads on the hotline yet?"

"Not that I've heard."

"It would be such a long shot to expect anyone to call in with a good lead. But we can always pray."

She smiled, the radiant smile that actually reached her eyes and lit them like pinpoints of liquid intensity, and his knees suddenly felt wobbly.

She arched an eyebrow. "You okay there?"

He couldn't form an answer, so he just nodded. "I'll be in the truck."

She chuckled. "Since when are you in a hurry if it didn't involve food, Special Agent Leebow?"

Since he started thinking of his best friend in such a different light. He grinned and snuck out the door. She had no idea what she did to his insides these days.

Chapter Eight

Milt tapped the table with his index finger. Where was she? He glanced out the window, over his shoulder, and then at the crinkled slip of paper. The code he and Olivia had set years ago indicated this Waffle House on this day. It was always their plan that she would leave a note for him, hidden in the panel in her closet that no one knew about.

What if she was hurt? What if her jaunt into the forest had truly gotten her lost? He swallowed, hard, and resumed his finger-tapping. He'd wait a little longer. If she didn't show, he'd retrace her possible steps. Probably should've started with that anyway. But that wasn't the plan, and Olivia knew what she was doing. Completely self-sufficient and competent.

He'd gone soft over the years. Each one that ticked by, the less diligent he'd been. He could smack himself for letting his guard down so much.

And now his sweet Olivia was in danger, of some sort, and he hadn't even seen it coming.

It had taken a long time to think of her as Olivia, but it suited her now. He closed his eyes and pictured the photos she'd managed to send him over the last five years. Not many. It was too risky. But he had treasured them more than any other assets in his life.

The crinkling of the booth seat behind him made his eyes snap open. His heart skipped for a second before he realized it wasn't her.

His coffee burned his throat. She wasn't coming.

"Tell me about court. Sorry I had to cut you off yesterday."

"Buchanan made a plea deal of some sort."

"Whoa. What must he know in order for them to offer him one?"

"I know. There was so much evidence against him."

Zach nodded.

Annalise took a deep breath and let it out slowly. She had him penned in the car, she might as well go for it. "What's up with you?"

"Me?" He grinned. "Nothing."

"I don't believe you. You've been weird the last couple days."

His smile fell. "I don't know."

"Zach? Since when do we have secrets?"

"This case is bothering me. Something made me think about my dad."

"Oh."

"Can we talk about something else?"

She squeezed his forearm. "For now, yes. But you're not getting off the hook forever. Just keep that in mind."

"I would expect nothing less from you Special Agent Baker."

Her mind drifted back to the Joanie, Olivia argument. "Let's swing by and follow up with the pharmacy before we head to headquarters. Now that we have the warrant."

Zach nodded.

"Do you think there's any way...no. Never mind." She bit her lip.

"What is it?"

"You don't think Olivia could be Joanie, do you?"

Zach furrowed his brow. "You were at her funeral, Annalise. You saw the evidence, the car, and the blood, and everything with your own eyes."

She was being paranoid. "You're right." She shook her head, but the thought wouldn't dislodge. "But, what if..."

"It's a conspiracy with a fake body in a real coffin?"

"Something like that, yes."

"How could we find out?"

She loved it that, even though she sounded nuts, Zach automatically jumped on her side. He would never dream of letting her pursue even the craziest idea alone. "Thanks, Zach."

"For what?"

"Being on my team."

"Always."

He swung into the pharmacy parking lot and they hopped out of his vehicle at the same time. Annalise led the way to the counter and pulled the warrant up on her tablet. She showed it and her badge to the man behind the counter. "We need to ask you some questions about Olivia Beck."

The pharmacist nodded.

"This pharmacy was listed as the family's primary." Actually, she'd seen the name on Jonah Beck's prescription bottles and noted it. "Do you have a record for Mrs. Olivia Beck?"

The pharmacist pecked at the keyboard. "Yes, officer."

"I need a printout of all activity on her account for the last six months, please."

The printer spurted to life behind him. She and Zach stared at him for a long, awkward moment until he handed the results to Annalise.

"Zach, look. She had a ninety-day prescription refilled three days ago."

"What for?"

"Blood pressure medicine."

"She left."

"Mmm-hmm."

"But why?"

"I don't know. It's time to ask Jonah some tough questions."

"I'll call Kirk."

When they arrived ten minutes later, Zach parked on the street in front of the Beck's home. "What if the kids are here?"

"Divide and conquer?"

Jonah frowned when he swung the door open. "Do you have any news?"

Zach shook his head. "We have a few questions."

"More questions, you mean. Haven't you asked enough already?"

Zach's tone grew more serious. "Are the children home, Mr. Beck?"

Watching from behind, with Jonah's attention on Zach, she caught the slight widening of Jonah's eyes, the paling of his cheeks.

"You know something, don't you?"

"Can we come in?"

Jonah nodded tersely and led them to the kitchen table. "What can I help you with?"

"Your wife's medicine is missing from the bathroom cupboard," Annalise began.

"I hadn't noticed."

"That's interesting, since your medicine is there too." Annalise questioned Jonah, but she knew Zach studied him intently, watching for the slightest hint of a lie.

"Wait, you went through our things? Don't you need a warrant for that?"

"You said I could take a look around yesterday. Remember?"

He dropped his head. "Yeah. I know." A huge sigh escaped him. "I'm scared. What if she doesn't come home? What do I tell the kids?" When he lifted his face, tears gleamed in his eyes.

Annalise's chest ached. "I'm sorry, Mr. Beck. We are doing everything we can." Had he processed yet what it meant that his wife had taken her medicine?

Zach cleared his throat.

"Mr. Beck, if your wife took her medicine with her, she had to be planning on leaving." She let it sink in for a moment.

Jonah's chest rose and fell, deeper with each inspiration.

"Can you think of any reason why she would want to do that?"

"It isn't poss…no…she wouldn't leave the children. Me, maybe."

"Why do you say that?"

"No marriage is perfect."

Didn't she know that so well? "Was there something in particular?"

He glanced away, his gaze darting to the wall behind her head and back.

"Nothing I can think of. She seemed happy. We were happy."

He wasn't being honest. Not completely. She would push later, if needed. "May I use your restroom, Mr. Beck?"

"Sure, just don't go through my stuff again." He smiled weakly.

"Right."

"You know where it is."

She nodded and excused herself from the table. Once out of sight, she slipped into the master bedroom and bath. As she hoped, long hairs dotted the brush on the counter. She cleaned it, stuffing the hairs into an evidence bag and tucking it into her pocket. Even if she turned out to be crazy, she had to follow this lead. Her mind would never rest until she knew for certain that Joanie was still deceased.

Chapter Nine

Zach stepped into the SMIF headquarters reception room behind Annalise. "Kirk?"

Kirk stepped from his office to the side. "Yeah?"

"Do you have financials on the Becks yet?"

"Yeah, hang on." Kirk disappeared back through his open door.

"I'm going out back for a bit," Annalise said, touching his elbow.

Tingles shot through his arm, much like when he hit his funny bone on something hard, only more pleasant. He stood staring after her and rubbing his elbow. That was new.

"Here you go."

Zach jumped and spun.

Kirk held out a file. "You okay?"

Nope. Not even a little bit. "Mm-hmm." He grabbed the folder and retreated to his office, shutting the door behind him.

He had to get his thoughts or hormones or whatever they were under control. This was Annalise he was thinking about. Best friends since sandbox days, newly divorced and vulnerable Annalise. No matter what he thought he felt, he had to tuck it away. Lock it inside a bulletproof case and throw it to the Mariana Trench.

He leafed through the Beck family's financials. They seemed to be in order. Why then couldn't he shake the feeling Jonah was hiding something? It was subtle. And it wasn't murderous—at least he didn't think so. But there was something.

Wait.

January 2019 outflows didn't match the rest of the months. There was a withdrawal of $2,500. Nowhere else did Zach see anything remotely close to that amount being removed. Maybe they'd bought new furniture or paid for a trip? But it merited further investigation. If Jonah would agree to answer questions again.

His phone beeped with an incoming text from his mom. He really needed to call her. But thoughts of his deadbeat, long-gone father kept pounding through his brain like an unwelcomed midnight train whistle. He and his mother hadn't spoken of Henry Leebow in more than a decade. It could wait another day. Or ten.

Decades.

At a knock on his door, he shut the file, both on his desk and in his mind. "Come in."

Annalise stepped through and sat across the desk from him. "I need to go to Memphis."

"Now?"

"I have to get the evidence from Joanie's case and compare the DNA from Olivia's hairbrush."

"Wait, what?"

Her voice dropped to a conspiratorial whisper, even though they were alone in his office. "I took hair from Olivia's brush when we were there earlier. I have to know if she and Joanie were related. Or if—" She shook her head. "I just have to do this."

"Okay. But wouldn't it be easier to request an evidence transfer?"

Her eyebrows wrinkled together over her nose. "Yeah, um, good idea."

"Look, Lise, I know you've been worried about your instincts since Dave left." He smiled. "But you have to trust them again. You have one of the most brilliant minds I've ever seen. If you have a hunch about something being off with these two people, I believe in you."

She beamed. "Thanks, Zach."

It was a good thing the desk sat between them. He had the sudden and almost overcoming urge to kiss the smile off her face. Also new.

Interesting.

"There's no way to get the evidence here now." She smiled and ducked her chin. "And now is when I want it."

He chuckled. Of course she did. Once Annalise Baker got an idea in her mind, she ran with it. Headlong, full-speed. Usually she was right though, so following her into battle was justified. Or anywhere for that matter. "If you put the request in now, it will only be a couple days."

"I know." She leaned back into her chair. "What's next?"

"One more aerial search, with a wider perimeter, is going out in about twenty minutes."

"You didn't want to be there?"

"Blu is handling it today." The subtle quirk of her lips poked him square in the ribs. "He promised to report in this evening."

"I hope they spot something."

"Me too. But I'm not holding my breath."

"Okay, well, I think I will drive over to see Paul. Maybe drive over to Olivia's school on the way back and see if her classroom can tell me anything new."

He nodded. "Good idea. I'm headed back to talk to Mr. Beck about the financials."

"Oh? Something interesting?"

"Maybe. A larger withdrawal than normal a few months back."

"Good catch."

His chest swelled. "Thanks. Be safe."

"Always." She paused at the door. "Wanna go see Buchanan with me tomorrow?"

"What? Why?"

"Call it another hunch."

"Count me in." He didn't need to know details. He'd follow her just about anywhere.

Annalise drew Paul into a hug as soon as the teen opened the door. She felt him stiffen, but she squeezed anyway. "It's good to see you, Paul."

He pulled back with a deep blush decorating his cheeks. "Thank you, ma'am. It's good to see you too."

She smiled as he rubbed his hand down his sleeve. This young man had won her heart from the day she met him, even if he was running from her at the time. Once she brought him home for protective detail and saw the vulnerability shining in his eyes, she couldn't hold his panicked flight against him. "Is the captain home?"

"No, he left early this morning, before I went to school."

"I'm so proud of you. Captain told me how amazing your grades have been this semester."

Paul's blush intensified. "Thank you."

"Do you know when he will be back?"

"Not sure."

"Well, I'll just try him on his cell after I leave. Can I come in?"

"Yeah, sure."

"I came to see you, Paul. Not just Captain Brooks."

"Oh." A sheepish grin broke out across his face. "Thank you, ma'am."

Paul closed the door and led her to the living room. "Do you want something to drink?"

"No, I'm fine. Really. I won't stay long. Tell me how things are. Catch me up."

"Um, good. Things are really good."

Annalise hadn't intended to make him uncomfortable, but she could tell by his squirming she had. "Need anything?"

"No, Mr. Brooks—Milt is taking care of everything for me."

"I'm so glad. You deserve someone like him, Paul. You really do."

"Thank you, ma'am."

She bit back a chuckle. Who would have thought the scrawny, disheveled, scared kid she met on his rickety porch steps six and a half months ago would turn into such a respectful, thankful kid calling her ma'am? "Have you heard from your brother?"

"I got a letter from Orrin this week. He says he is sorry every time he writes."

"You don't believe him?"

Paul shrugged. "I don't know what to believe. He left me behind that night. Cared more about himself than his kid brother."

"He made a mistake." Why she pushed him so hard to patch things up with his now-incarcerated brother, she wasn't so sure. All she knew was that she wanted him to.

An awkward silence hovered between them.

"I'll pray for you both. Maybe someday his apologies will hold some truth in them."

"Yeah, maybe."

"All right, I'll head out. Let Captain know I stopped by and need to talk to him, okay?"

"I will."

She embraced him one last time.

"He went to the mountains, Ms. Baker. Might be late when he gets home."

"Fishing again?"

"He didn't take any gear with him. Just a lunch and backpack."

That was weird. Captain Brooks didn't hike or do anything in the mountains other than fish, that she knew of.

When she reached her SUV, she dialed his number. It went straight to voicemail, and her stomach went straight to her toes. She had no reason to be suspicious of her ex-boss and still-friend, but she was.

Chapter Ten

Milt picked his way carefully along the trail above the Cades Cove picnic area. Call it a hunch, a premonition, an intuition, or madness, he needed to check something. Olivia's note had the code they'd prearranged: WH 35.98.-83.61.10. Waffle House, latitude, longitude, at ten AM. It had always been prearranged that they would meet the day after her disappearance.

But there was something else in the note. Something they hadn't discussed. A date, 06.14,69, only he would recognize as significant.

It could only mean one thing. Olivia wanted him at Spence Field, the location where a young boy had vanished without a trace on June 14, 1969. And the case that had intrigued Milt to the point of obsession. As a young adult, he'd hiked the forest off-trail more times than he could count, looking for a clue—any clue—to solve this mystery. A skeleton, an old tennis shoe. Anything that would tell what had happened to his distant relative. Anything that would explain why or how the boy could walk into the forest and disappear like smoke.

It couldn't be a coincidence that Olivia had chosen the same MO for her own escape plan. Nor could the date be nonviable information.

He stepped into the clearing. The waving of the grass changed with the direction of the breezes, a few logs dotted the landscape where before they hadn't, but Milt couldn't believe how vastly similar the landscape before him seemed. Memories rushed into the forefront of his mind. What must it have felt like to be one of those original men or women scrounging the area for the lost boy five decades ago? What must it have felt like to dedicate so much effort and time and come up completely, utterly empty handed?

A twinge shot through his chest. He knew Olivia had intentionally walked away from her family, that she wasn't lost and desperate for help, stranded somewhere in the dense Smoky Mountain forest. But he was letting some of his favorite people continue to believe she was.

He shook his head and corrected his monologue. Olivia was desperate for help, or she wouldn't have run. He couldn't let Annalise and Zach know yet the extent of his involvement in the case. Couldn't yet put their minds at ease. Not until he knew Olivia was safe.

He scoured the area, unsure what he was even looking for. The hikers and backpackers who had frequented this area took the "Leave no trace" motto seriously. There wasn't a single wrapper or piece of manmade anything anywhere.

Milt sank onto a log and sighed. Maybe he was wrong this time. But what else could Olivia's message to him mean?

He slipped his backpack off and grabbed a granola bar. His gaze traveled the height of the trees across the sheltered, grassy bald. Something bright flipped in a gentle breeze. What was that? He rose as quickly as his knees would allow and approached the far end of the field.

A yellow ribbon? It appeared to be snagged on a low limb, as if the tree had plucked it from some passerby's hair. He tugged it gently from the limb and inspected the back side. Safety pinned to its satiny top, a folded note waited, labeled simply "M."

His heart buoyed. Olivia. It had to be. His fingers shook as he undid the safety pin and opened the note to read it.

They found me. I will be fine. Keep my babies safe and tell Jonah I love him. The emergency stash is in a PO box below. Get it to them. Do not try to find me. It will only put you in danger.

Love,

O

Don't try to find her? Had she lost control of her senses? If they were after her again, he couldn't sit idly by and just hope for her safety. It was time to bring an end to this mess. Once and for all.

Annalise phoned the school ahead of time and arranged to meet with Principal Hughes. The soft-spoken woman had no problem with Annalise's idea to see Olivia's classroom.

"Whatever may help," Principal Hughes said as she shook Annalise's hand. "We are all terribly distraught. Olivia is such a kind, patient teacher. Her students just adore her."

Annalise's stomach constricted. The more she learned about Olivia, the more people she found that cared about her, the harder it was to admit they may never find her. She cleared her throat. "Can you show me to her classroom, please?"

"Yes, of course. Right this way."

Olivia's desk was tidy, as Annalise would've expected. Atop it, three pictures in one frame showed more smiling photos of the kids and Jonah. The light shining in Olivia's eyes in these photos matched the ones at their home. Genuine happiness and love for her family.

Annalise slipped an empty mug, stained with an internal coffee ring, into an evidence bag and sealed it. She could use it to match any fingerprints that may be in the evidence transferred from Memphis. Hopefully.

The walls of Olivia's classroom were decorated with everything she would've expected as well. Posters, maps, student artwork, and cheer. Annalise slid open each of Olivia's desk drawers but found nothing suspicious. She slumped into Olivia's squeaky chair. There was nothing here either.

If Olivia didn't want to be found, Annalise was starting to believe the woman wouldn't be.

Annalise paced the length of her living room.

Millie watched with droopy eyelids from her perch on the couch.

Three days until the evidence could make it from West Tennessee to East, and no leads whatsoever on Olivia's whereabouts.

She'd been in this position before. With Cody. A time or two in Memphis. No leads. No clues. She was missing something.

She checked her phone again. Still no call from Captain Brooks. Strange. Maybe he'd taken a personal day and was relaxing off-the-grid somewhere. Maybe he was hiding something.

The thought stopped her in her tracks. Again, for the millionth time, she reminded herself this was her friend she was talking about.

If only he would just call and put her mind at ease.

Her phone rang and she jumped to answer it. "Hello?"

"Hey, Lise. The search came up empty again. Blu and Kirk are officially calling it off with the bad weather that's moving in."

She glanced out the window. Perched high atop a mountain peak, her cabin gave her a terrific, nearly 360-degree view of the terrain below her. Sometime during her musings, dark, low-hanging clouds had moved in, obscuring the visibility and threatening a monster of a storm. Great.

Lord, please watch over Olivia. If she is out in this mess, she isn't safe.

Maybe she wasn't safe anyway. A woman like Olivia didn't seem the kind to traipse off, away from her family and her home and her job for nothing.

"I'm heading to see Jonah now about the financials. I'll call you when I finish."

"Sounds good. I'm going to continue making a rut in my floor."

"You'll figure it out. You always do."

"Thanks, Zach. Talk to you soon."

Her cabin felt even emptier as soon as the connection with Zach ended. Interesting.

Chapter Eleven

"Mr. Beck, may I come in?"

Jonah blocked the newly-opened door and crossed his arms over his chest. "Shouldn't you be out looking for my wife instead of here bugging me again?"

Slow raindrops began to plop onto Zach's exposed head. "The storm front moving in has forced our hand, sir."

Jonah huffed. "Of course it has."

Zach bit back a snarky retort. "I need to ask you about a $2,500 withdrawal in January."

Jonah's face drained of all color.

Good. Diving right in had caught the man off-guard. "Your family's finances aren't what they seem, are they, Jonah?"

Jonah swiped a shaky hand across his forehead. "Come in. I can explain."

Zach stepped into the family room.

Mr. Beck sank onto the couch and put his elbows on his knees. "I used to gamble. A lot. Before I met Olivia."

Zach nodded. "Go on."

"When we started dating, I gave that up. She made me want to be better, to be worthy of such an amazing woman. But last winter, I did something really stupid."

Zach quirked an eyebrow.

"We needed extra money for Christmas. I placed a few bets. And I lost. Big time."

"Did Mrs. Beck know?"

Jonah shook his head. "I didn't want to disappoint her."

"And the $2,500? Was that for another bet?"

"No, I used it to pay the balance. Olivia didn't know about that either. I thought the matter was over."

"But it wasn't?"

"A few weeks later I got a letter that I had outstanding interest balances." He chuckled mirthlessly. "One month doubled the amount I had borrowed to cover my debt. One month. The $2,500 wasn't enough to cover the interest."

"I'll need the name of the loaner you borrowed from."

"You won't tell Olivia, will you?" Jonah wrinkled his brow. "What am I saying? We don't even know where she is…"

Zach let the silence hover, pressing in around them and hopefully pressing out the rest of Jonah's truths.

"Have you…have there been any leads at all?"

Zach shook his head. "I'm sorry, Mr. Beck. We've had to call off the search with the storms moving in."

Jonah's chin fell to his chest. "I understand, but I sure don't like it."

Zach softened his tone. "Jonah, level with me here. Are you leaving anything out?"

"I got a threatening note. Just one. I dealt with it."

"Is there any chance Olivia's disappearance could be somehow related?"

"I don't see how. In March, they slashed my tire. I paid more on the debt."

"How have you been paying them?"

"Cash at a post office box." He pulled a key from his pocket. "Once a month."

"And you don't think Olivia noticed the missing money?"

"I took it from a bonus I earned. I do the finances. I don't think she figured it out."

Had Jonah ever planned on telling his wife? Zach mentally growled. Dishonesty, in any form, needled him. He'd spent too many years wondering about his father's secrets to appreciate any form of deceitfulness. He handed Jonah a pad of paper and pen. "Name and address of the loan agency and the post office."

Jonah complied, handing the notebook back with a scowl. "If this is my fault—"

"You lied to your wife, Mr. Beck."

Jonah shrank farther into the couch cushions.

Zach shouldn't have said that. Very unprofessional of him. He opened his mouth to apologize but found the word wouldn't form. He'd meant it. Dave had lied to Annalise too, and she hadn't deserved it. He doubted very highly Olivia did either. "All right, I'll check these out. Next time I come with more questions, don't get an attitude."

"Yes, sir." Jonah sighed. "You know, I've been thinking. Olivia sometimes kept her blood pressure medicine with her, just in case we were out past time for her to take it. Maybe she didn't plan…didn't plan on leaving me, as you implied."

The man had a good point, but it didn't help much. "I'll make a note of it." If they took the assumption that Olivia had intentionally left back off the table, it only opened more avenues.

Zach excused himself and aimed his truck for town.

Annalise pulled into the gravel parking lot at Quick Loans and waved at Zach. His new discovery was the first time she'd felt any excitement yet.

"You're so smart," she praised as she rounded the hood and smiled at him.

"Hey, I could've told you that." Zach grinned.

She punched his shoulder. "You have. Multiple times."

"'Bout time you listened."

She rolled her eyes. "Let's go, Einstein."

Zach held the door for her, sliding around and approaching the counter first. "You recognize this man," he asked the kid behind the counter.

Creative business name these guys had come up with. And the décor. So cliché. Annalise studied the boy as he decided how to answer Zach's question. His eyes widened slightly. He recognized Jonah. She nudged Zach's elbow, giving him the affirmative signal.

"Good, young man. Now, tell me about the...methods...you've used to extract payment."

Panic filled the boy's eyes. He threw his hands up in surrender. "I know nothing, mister. I swear. I just work the desk. Let me get Harley."

Annalise stifled a grin. That was easy.

"By all means, please, show us to the man who can tell us."

The kid sent a quick text.

Moments later a tall, thin man with a thick, gray beard entered through a curtain to the rear. "How may I help you, officers?"

"Special Agents Leebow and Baker." Zach showed his badge, and Annalise did the same. "We have some questions about a client of yours. Jonah Beck."

The man raked three fingers through his beard. "Doesn't sound familiar."

"Let me help you remember." Zach flashed his best fake smile and held his phone toward the man. "Jonah Beck. Father of two. Husband of one. Made some stupid mistakes first of the year. You decided to charge him egregious amounts of interest and slash his tires when he couldn't pay. Sound familiar?"

The man returned Zach's fake smile. "Not a word."

Annalise picked up on the twitch of the man's chin. He, obviously, was lying.

"Now, unless you have a warrant, I'd ask you to leave."

Zach took four steps toward the man and leaned in close.

Annalise's heart bottomed out. Not the time or place to get physical, Zachary Leebow. She held her breath and her motions perfectly still, watching the boy. Just in case.

"A woman is missing. The mother of those two children. If we find out you had something to do with it, tire slashing is going to seem like child's play. Understand?"

The man's grin widened. "Call the cops, J.C. I want to report a threat from this *special agent*."

The boy lifted his phone.

Annalise grabbed Zach's arm and dragged him from the building. "That's enough. What has gotten into you?"

He shrugged her hand off. "Nothing."

She snorted. "Oh, yeah right. Come on. We need to talk." She ushered him to his truck. "Follow me."

"Yes, ma'am."

The cloud had lifted from his eyes and the playful spunk she was used to shone through. "I'm serious, Zach."

"On your six."

She drove to the Waffle House near I-75 and waited for him to pull into the parking lot a few minutes later. She'd lost him a few stop lights back, but he knew where she'd head. It was always their talking place.

He stepped from the truck with a smile, but she could tell by the way he wouldn't square his body toward her that he was nervous about the confrontation. Something must really be bothering him. "I need a peanut butter chip waffle and ten pieces of bacon."

"Sounds good."

Not his usual response to the promise of food.

Once in the booth, with cups of steaming coffee between them, Annalise leveled a stern gaze. "Spill."

"Don't wanna."

He sounded like the boy she knew from their childhood with his nasally whine. "Too bad."

"I…this case made me think of my dad."

Whoa. This was big. And she had been right.

"Cat got your tongue?"

"I'm sorry, Zach. Thank you for telling me."

"He disappeared too. Walked right out of my life. And for what? Another woman? To be a bachelor? To just disappear and be selfish and see the world? I'll never know, and it makes me angry. Really angry."

"That's not necessarily true. You've never talked to your mom about it, have you?"

He shook his head, his shoulders sinking a few more millimeters.

"What if she has answers and you just don't know it because you couldn't bring yourself to ask?"

"I don't want to hurt her."

"Your dad hurt her, Zach. Not you. How do you know she isn't dying to talk to you about it?"

"She isn't."

"We're going there after we eat."

He jerked his gaze back to her. "What? No way."

Now he sounded like the argumentative, whiny teenager he'd once been. Staring into his vivid-green eyes, though, she quickly realized he was far from it. With his thick, stiff-set lips and bulging vein running down the side of his neck, images of the boy vanished, replaced by the man sitting in front of her now. Something fluttered deep within her abdomen. Just a tiny little wing flipping. Once, twice.

What. Was. That?

Chapter Twelve

"Annalise! What a wonderful surprise."

Zach's mother wrapped her arms around Annalise's neck and squeezed. "Come in, dear. I just made no-bake cookies."

"You'll spoil me, Lorraine."

"Hasn't happened yet, has it?"

Annalise chuckled. "No, I suppose not."

"I'm here too, Mom."

Lorraine released her and tugged her son into an embrace. "Of course you are, baby. I would never forget about you."

Lorraine's placating tone made Annalise smile. She knew her boy very well.

"How long has it been, Annalise dear?"

"Too long."

Lorraine looped one arm through each of theirs and pulled them through the storm door into the warm, sweet-smelling kitchen. "Sit down. Tell me what brings you both by on a weekday afternoon."

Zach pinned Annalise with a look she was sure she'd hear the words behind later. Something about her stubbornness and bossiness, no doubt.

Lorraine poured coffee and set out a plate of still-gooey cookies.

"Mmmm, I haven't had these in forever," Annalise said as she tucked herself onto a barstool at the island.

"Mom, I just wanted to check on you."

It sounded lame even to Zach, Annalise would bet. She rolled her eyes and glared at him with her own underlying-meaning gaze. "We wanted to ask you about Zach's father."

The coffee pot fell from Lorraine's hand and clanked against the counter, shattering into a million pieces all over the tile.

Well, that went well. Not. "Lorraine, I am so sorry."

"I told you to let it lie, Annalise." Zach stormed out of the room one way and Lorraine, the other.

"I'll just clean this up, I guess," Annalise said to no one. She'd known Zach and Lorraine all her life, it seemed. She'd never seen them act this way before. How was she supposed to know it would touch such a nerve?

Okay, that wasn't true. She knew it was a tender subject, but she thought they'd all be grownups about it. Further proof her instincts weren't as on-point as she'd like at the moment. Stupid Dave and his mistress and criticisms of Annalise and self-doubt and guilt...the list could go on for miles.

Annalise got the broom and dust pan from the pantry and a roll of paper towels and tried to sop up the disaster. "Ouch!" Dropping the broom, she squeezed her thumb between the opposite forefinger and thumb as blood bubbled up in a big blob. Great.

She rushed to the sink and held her thumb under the cool water. As soon as the blood slowed, she plucked unsuccessfully at the sliver of glass wedged in her flesh.

Zach's arms slid around her and stilled her hands. "Let me."

Gooseflesh raced up her arms and down her back. She squeezed her eyes tight and leaned back into his chest.

"There."

Her eyes flew open. "You got it already?"

"Yep. Here," he wrapped a paper towel around her still-oozing thumb. "Let me get a Band-Aid."

When Zach walked away, Annalise let out the breath she'd been holding. What was happening to her? She'd been officially divorced for only a few days. And this was Zach. Her emotions weren't playing nice tricks on her.

He returned a moment later, and Annalise took the bandage from him. No sense risking flutters or chill bumps again. "Thanks."

"Can we go now? I told you this was a bad idea."

"I know you did. I'm sorry. I have always hoped you'd find out what happened to him. I guess my imagination version of this long-lost reunion isn't realistic."

"I never said I wanted a reunion."

She dropped her chin a notch. "No, you're right. You didn't."

"Here."

Annalise and Zach both spun to face Lorraine.

She laid a box on the table and, without another glance or word, retreated once more from the kitchen.

Annalise raised her eyebrow and looked at Zach. "What do you suppose is in there?"

"Dunno. Never seen it before."

Zach picked it up, inspected every outside surface, and set it back down.

"You're stalling."

He sank into a chair. "What if I don't really want to know what's in there?"

Annalise frowned. "You do, Zach. You know you do." She inched the box closer to him and smiled. "I'm here. No matter what's inside."

He lifted the lid with a shaky hand and peered inside.

What was it? What made his eyes round and his nostrils flare? She bit her lip to give him the silence for processing that he needed. But it wasn't easy.

When he lifted his gaze, his eyes shone with unshed tears. He held up an envelope and showed her the front. *To Zach. If he ever asks about me. ~Dad*

Annalise gasped. "Are you going to open it?"

"I…I don't know."

"Could be the answers you want."

"Could be more questions."

"Only one way to find out."

He drew a deep breath. "You open it." And thrust the envelope in her hand.

"What? No, I can't do this for you."

"Why not? You asked Mom for me. You made me come today."

The tone in his voice stung her deepest heartstrings, like jellyfish tentacles wrapping her emotions in them and squeezing. "I didn't make you. I can't make you do anything, Mr. Bullheaded."

Annalise dropped the envelope on the table and let the storm door slam behind her. When he was thinking more clearly, she'd sort this out with him. Maybe, too, when she wasn't about to burst into tears.

Captain Brooks silenced his phone as another text from Annalise beeped in. He wasn't ready to talk yet.

The photos, documents, court transcripts, and other items in his personal evidence collection littered the desk in front of him. How many times in five years had he scoured these same pieces of paper? And how many times had he found no new answers?

Senator Marcum was behind bars. The case closed. Yet, the real truth, the real mastermind behind the scenes had never been caught. As far as he knew, he was the only one still looking. Better for Annalise if she never knew the depth of the drug ring she'd help bring down in Memphis. Better for him if she never realized his level of involvement.

But, boy, he sure could use her amazing mind. If he revealed all the details he knew, would she be able to see something he hadn't before?

If Olivia was scared enough to disappear, though, it meant anyone he brought in would be in danger. He couldn't risk Annalise's life to the Juarez cartel again. He hadn't known her very well the first time they'd all dealt with this case, observing her only from behind the scenes. Now that he knew her personally, he definitely couldn't take big chances. Not unless he had to.

Frustration hammered against his ribs along with his heartbeat. The same frustration he'd faced for so many years now. Senator Marcum sat uncomfortably behind bars, Annalise's testimony sealing his fate for the next thirty years. The Juarez drug ring had busted up shortly thereafter.

Why, then, did Olivia word her note the way she had? *They found me.* There could only be one they. Someone had taken the reins.

And they would kill her for what she'd seen.

Olivia jerked upright. The cheap hotel bed squeaked its annoyance. In the pitch black of her rented room, for a moment she forgot where she was and reached a hand to feel the warmth of Jonah's strong shoulders. His side of the bed was cold. And hadn't been warm to start with.

She sighed and flopped back onto the pillow, tears leaking from the corners of her eyes.

The nightmare still played behind the veil of darkness. Once she'd married Jonah, the horrible half-truths had faded. It seemed they were back in full force.

The screams. That's what got her. Listening to the young woman's agonizing screams and being unable to do a thing to help her. Watching helplessly from the shadows while the Juarez underlings tortured her to the point of insanity.

Knowing she herself would be next.

Knowing neither of them was leaving that warehouse, even if they gave the information the thugs wanted.

Olivia had known the risks of diving headfirst undercover into the toughest drug cartel in Memphis. Had known the side effects of pretending to fall for one of their men, of being something she wasn't and compromising her moral compass for her job.

Until that very moment, none of it had seemed a real possibility. Oh, how wrong she had been.

In the nightmare, she could taste the coppery blood and feel the physical force of Maria's death.

In real life, it was her own blood she'd tasted from biting her tongue to keep from crying out, but the impact of Maria's death had been reality. Olivia shivered.

If they found her, this time there would be no escape. No new identity. No plastic surgery and fake background history. No starting over. No safety for her husband and children.

She had to keep moving.

To put as much distance between herself and the Juarez cartel as possible.

Regret the size of a jousting lance pierced her heart and stole her breath. She curled into the fetal position under the covers and pictured her babies's faces. She'd never see them again. Annalise would continue thinking she was dead. Jonah would think she'd left him.

But if the Juarez men had followed her from Memphis to Knoxville, they would follow her anywhere they could find her. She couldn't let that happen again.

As dawn lit the curtained window, she dried her tears and crawled from her nest of sorrow. Enough of that. For all she knew, while she laid in her tears, they were closing in. They thought she knew too much. Thought she'd seen who wore the big boots in the operation. They didn't believe her when she told them the truth. She'd seen nothing but the life ebbing from Maria's dark eyes.

Chapter Thirteen

"Buchanan." Zach practically growled the three syllables.

Annalise patted Zach's forearm. "Easy, tiger."

Buchanan grinned as he took the bench across from them. "So good to see you fine officers again."

Her nostrils flared as she bit back a sharp retort. "Oh, yes, you too." Her sarcasm wasn't a tiny bit veiled. "We need to chat."

"Oh? Whatever about?"

She was going to slap him. No doubt about it. Before their short visit was over, her hand, or maybe fist, was going to connect with his ugly face.

Touching hers under the table, Zach's thigh tensed.

He was definitely having a hard time holding back too.

"Listen, Buchanan. We know you have some powerful information that's keeping you alive."

His smile fell. "Not allowed to talk about it. You should know that."

She suspected as much. "Fine. You don't talk. You just listen."

Zach picked up the thought, as if they'd rehearsed it all. "Here's what we think. You just give us a little nod if we get close to the truth."

Annalise folded her hands on the tabletop. "You rolled. Hard. On someone very powerful."

"And in turn for your testimony or implications or just information, you get to live."

"Assuming the men you rolled on don't find out."

Buchanan simply smiled.

But Annalise wasn't watching his mouth. She was watching his left eye twitch. Ever so slightly with each statement. "Let's go through the list. See if we can hit the nail on the head. Zach?"

"My pleasure. Jamison Branch?"

Annalise figured Zach would start with the more infamous moonshiners. But the first name elicited no twitch.

"Hammer boys."

Nothing.

"Hentons."

Nada.

"Smythe and Roberts."

Zach switched to drug runners. Still nothing.

"Juarez."

Buchanan's left eyelid flicked. Ah. That was it. Annalise's stomach dropped. She swallowed hard. "The Juarez Cartel is active again."

Buchanan's eyelid again gave him away.

"They are here in Knoxville."

Twitch.

Annalise's dropped stomach leaped back into her throat. She'd suspected the Juarez's had relocated, but to know the group was here…she shuddered. The men who burned down her home and killed Joanie were too close for comfort.

"Thanks, Buchanan. We'll be in touch." Zach rose to leave.

"But I didn't say nothing." Buchanan's voice suddenly seemed higher. "Tell them I didn't say nothing."

"You didn't have to." Annalise forced a semblance of a smile.

"They'll kill me."

"Who?"

Buchanan clamped his lips tight.

Annalise dropped her voice to a whisper. "You were dead already, rolling on them. The Juarez's don't leave loose ends."

The blood drained from Buchanan's face.

"Come on, Annalise." Zach gently tugged her to her feet.

She shrugged off his hand and followed him through the many corridors and locked doors, feeling like a zombie all the way out and back to her SUV. She left without telling Zach goodbye.

If Olivia was really Joanie, and if the Juarez cartel was truly here in Knoxville, could they have something to do with her disappearance? Annalise shivered again. Though she didn't want to admit it, it was the best possibility.

Or worst, depending on how she looked at it.

"Delivery for you, Annalise!" Zach's voice floated through her open office door.

Yes. Joanie's evidence boxes had arrived. She wore a broad smile when she entered the lobby. Perhaps this would be good enough distraction from her visit with Buchanan that she could stop obsessively revolving the same fears and worries over and over and over.

Zach helped her carry them into her office. "Wow. More than I thought. Where will you start?"

"Umm, in box number one, I suppose." A giant purple dragon of awkwardness hovered between them. They hadn't spoken at the jail of their argument. They hadn't spoken much at all, in fact.

He chuckled, but it sounded forced. "Sounds logical to me."

When had they last had any type of argument? Annalise hadn't slept much last night worrying about him. She was still mad, but it was time to offer an olive branch. In light of Buchanan's information, she had bigger dragons to slay anyway.

She needed her friend. She thrust the box's lid into his outstretched hand. "Wanna help?"

"Of course." He smiled, a genuine one this time.

For the next three hours they dug through each box. Annalise retrieved a DNA sample and packed it with the hair from the Beck's and sent them out to the lab for comparison. Part of her hoped they matched. The other ninety percent of her wondered what the ramifications would be if they did.

"Look, Annalise." Zach broke into her thoughts.

"Hmm?"

"I'm sorry."

"I know. Open the envelope yet?"

"No."

"I'm sorry I pushed before you were ready. I don't like seeing you so upset."

"I know. How many times have you gone through these boxes?"

"More than I can count. But it's been years."

"Anything triggering anything?"

She shook her head and pulled the last slip of paper from the fourth box. Her stomach knotted. "Zach, oh my gosh. Look."

Captain Brooks's signature stood out on the evidence log as bright as an airport landing strip. She handed the paper to him and sank back into her chair. How could Captain Brooks be involved in the case that had changed her life and she not know about it? How could he not tell her? At any point during her time working for him, why would he not come clean about it?

"Look, Annalise, maybe he couldn't. Maybe his role was more classified than we realize."

"But...but—"

"You worked with him for what almost three years?"

She nodded.

"If he could have told you, he would have."

"How can you be so sure?"

"He's one of the good guys."

She lifted her eyebrow. "Same question."

"Annalise, you know him. You've seen him in action, seen his integrity."

She'd seen Dave too. Every day for nine years. She hadn't expected his affair, his betrayal, his harsh words. "I need some air."

"I need to go to the post office and see if I can get information on Jonah's box. Want to join me?"

With a hand pressed to her stomach, Annalise shook her head. She made her way to her garden oasis. She should've brought Millie today. She could use the reassurance and calm her beloved beagle brought her.

Zach showed Jonah's photo to the post office supervisor. "Do you recognize this man?"

The woman, Audrey according to her nametag, shook her head. "He seems kind of familiar but nothing that specifically stands out."

"We suspect he was being blackmailed through a P.O. box at this location. Have you noticed any suspicious activity, or maybe had any customers that made you feel uncomfortable?"

"Not really, no. I'm sorry."

"That's okay. Here is my business card. If you think of anything, please do not hesitate to call." Zach smiled warmly, hoping to leave a good impression in her mind.

He returned to his truck at the curb and slid behind the wheel. Would they actually catch any breaks in this frustrating case? *Lord, I don't know what to do.*

Whoa. How many days had it been since he'd last prayed? This case, and especially this thing with his dad, had thrown him off.

Maybe he should just open the envelope right now. See what his dear old dad wanted to tell him. He snickered. Right. He'd gone this long without knowing. What difference could it possibly make now? The man had left him and Mom, walked from their lives and never looked back. Nothing he could say would make that easier to swallow.

Zach tapped the steering wheel with his thumb and stared at the front door of the post office. He dialed Jonah. "Mr. Beck, when was the next payment due?"

"Tomorrow."

"Perfect. Thanks."

Tomorrow, he and Annalise would stake out the post office, while Kirk tied up some loose ends from another case. If something didn't break soon, they'd be forced to put Olivia Beck in the unsolved, on-hold, grimace-every-time-they-looked-at-the-file category. It would drive all of them mad having a case with no answers so soon after their new task force had been formed.

In the last seven months, they had solved Cody Moss's kidnapping and put Jimmy Vern behind bars. They had officially shut down the Moonshine Mafia Jimmy Vern led too. They'd solved a murder in Gatlinburg, an automobile theft in Pigeon Forge, and tracked down a lost group of Boy Scouts. So far, so good.

Until now.

Until Olivia Beck walked into the forest, possibly of her own free will, and decided to vanish. Maybe this wasn't a case they were meant to solve. Maybe she had good reason to leave. She was sick of Jonah's gambling or something had just snapped in her mind.

Who understood why a normal, sane person walked away from their family?

He dropped his forehead to the steering wheel. His mind was not playing kindly with him lately. He had to stop obsessing. Annalise may be right. He should open the envelope and get it over with.

His hands shook as he retrieved it from the glove box. He stared at it for a good, long while before stuffing it back in. Nope. Not ready yet.

Chapter Fourteen

"Do you really think he'll show up?" Annalise munched a cinnamon crunch bagel and leaned on the passenger windowsill.

Zach held back a grin. Annalise was already ready to spring from the vehicle. "Yeah. Maybe."

"I'm bored."

Ha! Yep. He chuckled. "Why am I not surprised? We've been sitting here for an hour, so you've made it pretty long."

She punched his shoulder. "Whatever."

If he could get her thinking about something else, she'd be able to be more patient. "When do the DNA results come in?"

"It could be a while. Wasn't exactly a priority."

"Yeah."

"You open the envelope yet?"

His stomach turned over as he popped the glove box open. "Nope."

"Why not?"

Terrible, debilitating fear that made him sweat and stumble just thinking about it. "Dunno."

"Right." She snorted.

Zach's gaze followed the loan shop owner's footsteps as he paused at the post office door, scanned the parking lot, and then turned to enter the building. "Annalise, there." He pointed. "He's here."

She sat up straighter. "Plan?"

"Let's give him a minute to open the box, then we corner him."

"Deal."

They exited the truck simultaneously and paused at the front door. Zach counted to thirty, then entered with his hand on the butt of his gun. He sensed Annalise's presence behind him. He stopped inside the door, shifted to the right, and scanned the lobby. Where had Harley gone?

Annalise nudged his side.

He trailed her gaze.

Harley stepped from the door leading to the rear of the post office. With a gun held to the supervisor's head and an arm around her neck. "Hi, officers."

Zach swallowed. "Harley, you don't want to do this."

"Put your guns down, and she lives."

"Easy, Harley. We just wanted to ask you some more questions." Zach tightened his grip.

"Right. Well, ask away."

Audrey's eyes widened even farther.

Had Harley tightened his grip around her windpipe? Pressed the gun harder against her temple? Zach took a step back and lowered his gun fractionally. "Easy, Harley."

"Put the gun down, Harley. Let her go." Annalise conveyed what Zach liked to call her puppy tone. He'd seen her rear Millie with it, and it worked to calm panicked criminals and victims alike. Usually.

Harley just smiled. "I'm leaving, one way or another. You two decide if it will be as a murderer or simply a blackmailer."

Zach had a feeling there were other crimes already on that list too. "Okay, look I'm putting my gun down." He bent ever-so-slowly and laid the gun on the floor. "Let Audrey go."

Annalise followed his lead, though he felt the tenseness in her shoulder as she brushed his arm.

Harley shoved Audrey to the floor and fired a quick round in Zach and Annalise's direction.

They dove to the tile and a millisecond later the window behind them shattered into a million tiny, blue-green pieces.

"Are you okay?" He rose onto his knees and hovered over Annalise.

She rolled onto her back and stared up at him with his huge pupils. She nodded. "I'm fine. Go get him."

Zach kissed her forehead quickly and sprinted toward the back, where Harley had disappeared.

Annalise leaped to her feet and raced through the front door. Left or right? Left or right? Harley had approached from the left. She dashed in that direction and rounded the building. At the back corner, she paused, pulled her weapon to her shoulder, and peeked around. Nothing. No sign of Zach or Harley, but the back door swung on its hinges.

Where had they gone?

A gunshot splintered the air.

Her stomach plummeted. *Please, Lord, don't let Zach be on the receiving end of that.*

She followed the sound, cautiously rounding each building. She pulled to a stop, gasping as she spotted Zach tangled on the ground with Harley. She took ten seconds to catch her breath and calm her shaking hands, then stepped out and approached with confident steps. "Hands up, Harley."

The tussle instantly froze.

Before she blinked, Zach had rolled away from Harley and was standing next to her. "Thanks, partner."

"My pleasure. Can't have you coming to work shot or dead, you know."

"Would be very hard to do dead."

"You're under arrest, Harley. Roll over."

Harley complied, and Zach handcuffed him. He yanked the dejected man to his feet and led him back to Zach's vehicle.

It would be an entertaining ride taking Harley back on the bench seat between them. But she couldn't wait to let Kirk at him.

Annalise crossed her arms over her chest and stared through the one-way glass.

Harley shifted in his hard, plastic chair again, though he tried to portray calm.

It wasn't fooling her. And it wouldn't fool Kirk. Where was he anyway? The longer Harley sat in there, collecting his thoughts and straightening his story, the more likely he was to ask for a lawyer. Because there was no doubt in her mind he had crimes. Whether they were related to Olivia Beck or not remained to be seen.

The door in the interrogation room opened, and Kirk entered.

Finally. Annalise sighed.

He sat across the table from Harley and busied himself flipping slowly through a thick file.

"Listen, man. This is all a mistake." Harley fiddled with his water bottle.

Kirk didn't look up or act like he'd even heard the man.

"I got a lot of enemies, some's where badges."

Still, Kirk leafed through papers.

"I panicked. Okay? Better safe than sorry, you know." Harley chuckled and shifted in his seat.

"This is Jonah Beck's wife, Olivia." Kirk slid an eight by ten photo across the table. "She's missing. You know where she is."

Harley smiled for a millisecond and then must have realized Kirk wasn't joking. "Wait, what? No. No, I have nothing to do with that."

Kirk folded his hands on the tabletop and pinned Harley with a steady gaze.

"I swear. Jonah owes me money. That's it."

"You threatened him."

"Aw, please. My threats are just that, empty threats. Are you crazy? Why would I risk jail for a couple thousand bucks?"

The man had a point there.

"You tell me, Harley. So far today you've assaulted federal officers, ran from those same officers, and sat here pretending like you aren't in a big pile of trouble. Not much of what you do makes sense to me, so enlighten us."

"Look, man, I swear. I know nothing, zip, zero, zilch, nada about a missing woman. I did, I admit it, blackmail Jonah. But that's it. I'm a business man. I saw an opportunity and took it."

"How many other customers are you taking advantage of with your upstanding business practices, Harley?"

"I...uh...you know what, it's time to call a lawyer. Now." He leaned back in his chair and clenched his jaw firmly shut.

"Of course." Kirk exited the room.

Great. Well, at least he talked before he clammed up. Problem was, Annalise believed Harley. He wasn't involved in Olivia's disappearance. Time to call the lab and see if she could encourage them to hurry.

Back at her desk, she dialed their number. "I need to check on the status of a couple samples I sent in for comparison, please." She relayed the case number to the technician.

"I'm sorry, ma'am, I don't see anything registered under that number."

"I sent it in day before yesterday. Under Special Agent Baker, from Sevierville."

"Hmm, no. I'm still not seeing anything. I'm sorry."

"How—" What was happening? How had two samples gone completely missing?

"Can I help you with anything else?"

"I need you to try again. I know the samples made it there. I checked on them myself."

"I don't know what to tell you, Special Agent. They aren't here now."

Annalise's rock-heavy stomach burned as she hung up.

Annalise handed him a mug of hot chocolate and perched on the edge of her couch. "They're gone, Zach. Gone."

Zach patted her knee and quickly withdrew his hand, wrapping them both around his mug instead. "The lab doesn't lose samples."

She fiddled with her coffee cup and stared at the fire in her hearth. "I know."

"Something about this whole situation gives me a bad feeling." And something about the tingling in his palm gave him a strange feeling he couldn't explain.

"Me too."

Millie's head lifted, her ears perked toward the front door.

Annalise and Zach both turned their gazes toward it.

Millie growled.

No knock sounded.

"That's weird. She never growls at the door unless someone is there." Annalise set her mug on the table and rose.

"Hang on, I'll check it out." Zach mirrored her movements. "Stay here."

"Oh, yeah right."

He snickered. Why had he expected that to work? He claimed the window to the right of the front door, Annalise the one to the left. "See anything?"

Millie, now on her feet, let out another low rumble.

"No," Annalise whispered. "You?"

"No." He drew his weapon and turned the knob slowly. "Be right back."

"I'm coming." She pinned him with a fierce glare as she pulled her backup weapon from the drawer safe next to the door.

He knew better than to argue. He slid the door open silently.

Millie dashed past him.

"Millie, no," Annalise hissed. "What if it's a bear?" She darted after her pet.

Zach wanted to follow, but something made the hairs on the back of his neck stand erect. From the front porch step, he peered into the night. The sounds of Annalise's footsteps and the rustling of Millie's paws in the leftover leaves reached him from the west. No night birds or frogs sounded, casting the night in an eerie silence.

He grabbed the spotlight from behind his truck seat and shined it into the trees. Nothing reflected back to him other than trunks, underbrush, and grass, but he couldn't help feeling something, or someone, was watching him back.

"Annalise!"

"Yeah!" Her voice came to him from around the corner of her cabin.

He backed to the house, keeping the spotlight shining into the forest, and then made his way around to her. "You find Millie?"

"No. It isn't like her to take off like this."

"You getting the feeling we aren't alone?"

"Yes." Annalise shivered.

He released the button on the spotlight, fading them into darkness. After a few moments to let his eyes adjust, he nudged her side. "Come on. She will come back, and I would feel better getting you back inside."

"I can take care of myself, Zach."

"Always could." But he sorely wanted to be the one to carry that responsibility now. He pulled her to the front door and, with one last glance behind him, shut and locked it.

"I'm getting some food."

"I can always eat."

"Not for you. For Millie." Annalise filled the dog's bowl and stepped out onto the rear deck.

This woman! Hadn't he just brought her inside, away from whatever it was outside that made him feel so squirmy?

Millie entered the back door, followed by a smiling Annalise.

Zach sighed. "All clear now?"

"Seems to be but…" Annalise shut the door and locked it behind her.

"I feel it too." He holstered his gun. "I'm staying tonight."

"Zach, really, you don't have to do that."

"Try and make me leave."

She held her hands up in surrender. "I wouldn't dare."

The sly grin she flashed his way made his stomach somersault. He cleared his throat. "I'll take the couch."

"I have a guest bedroom."

Yeah, but it was closer to hers. "The couch will be fine. I can keep an eye on the front and back doors that way."

"Suit yourself."

"I'll scope out the perimeter in the morning."

"Yeah, and then we have to figure out why my samples went missing."

"Or who caused them to disappear."

"Exactly."

Chapter Fifteen

Annalise sighed as Zach reentered the front door of her cabin and sat at the kitchen barstool. "There's nothing there."

"Yeah. I kind of didn't think there would be."

"I still can't shake the feeling someone was there."

Zach had been scouring the edges of her property for over an hour as the morning sun rose above the canopy of full leaves. Meanwhile, she'd been scouring the online submission records of her case. It hadn't taken long. There weren't any.

She handed him a plate of bacon and eggs and sat across from him. "Someone deleted every trace of the samples I sent, Zach."

"Who would do that? And why?"

She bit her lip. "The entire case against Senator Marcum was 'resolved,' but I never really thought it was. Remember?"

"How could I forget, Lise? You nearly ruined yourself looking for proof of Joanie's murder."

"I know you know, I'm just thinking out loud, I guess."

"By all means, please continue." He grinned. "And ask the question that's burning your mind."

"Do you think Milt is involved?"

He scratched his stubbly chin, sprinkled with just a touch of gray these days. "I trust him."

"I thought I did too." But she had trusted Dave.

"He isn't like Dave."

"Ugh." She dropped her chin to her palm. "Get out of my head."

"I like it in there." He raised one eyebrow.

She rolled her eyes.

"It's this beautiful mess of intelligence and emotion and worry and fear and bravery and honesty and…"

With each new adjective, his voice had dropped until he nearly whispered the last and. Her voice matched his when she found the will to speak. "And what?"

He shook his head. "Come on, let's go to the lab ourselves. We can ask Scott to dig into the system and see where the deletion keystrokes came from. In theory anyway."

What word was he leaving out? It would drive her crazy, but something told her not to push.

Something told her she wasn't sure she wanted to know. Whatever it was might change everything. "Okay, let's go."

They dropped their plates into the dishwasher and aimed for the lab in Knoxville.

Scott worked on pulling up the login history from the last twenty-four hours, while Annalise drummed her fingers on the edge of his desk.

Fifteen minutes felt like an eternity.

"I can't exactly trace who did what once they were in the system, but I can tell you who logged in and you can cross-reference active case entries with those names. You should be able to narrow it down."

"One name will have no case," Zach said from behind her.

"That's the idea."

"But not a foolproof plan, because someone could have logged in to check something and not started a new case entry." Annalise sighed.

"Right." Scott hit a series of keys, and the printer to his left came to life. He handed it to her.

She scanned the list and compared it to the next page he handed her of new entries. Her heart dropped. "It can't be a coincidence," she said as she handed the pages to Zach.

He read over them and frowned. "Don't jump to conclusions yet."

"He'd better be available. Milt's been dodging me for days."

Scott's eyebrows rose, but he didn't comment.

"Thanks, man." Zach shook his hand, and they turned to go.

They shot up the interstate and parked at the Norris Police Department's picturesque front entrance.

"Take a deep breath, Annalise."

She did as Zach instructed. "What if—"

"Talk to him first."

She tried to quiet the anxiety roiling in her mind and stomach, but it wasn't working very well. She burst into Captains Brooks's office.

He jerked his gaze toward her and then smiled. "Hey, guys. What brings you over?"

"We need to talk. You haven't answered my calls or messages for two days."

"Been busy."

Was he trying to pacify her? He was using his "calm-down-hyped-up victim" voice.

Zach shut the door behind them. "This is serious, Milt."

"You know."

It was not a question, nor was there a hint of guilt, but Annalise's heart thundered to life. "Know what, Captain?"

"I erased the evidence you submitted, Annalise. I have flagged her case for any new activity. When you submitted the samples, I was alerted, and I dealt with it."

She expected it, but it still felt like someone punched her in the gut. "Why would you do that?"

"It's complicated."

Zach put a reassuring hand on her shoulder. "I think you'd better tell us everything."

"Olivia Beck didn't vanish."

Annalise sank into a chair, finding her legs no longer willing to support her.

Zach took the one beside her.

"She walked away to protect her family. The Senator Marcum case, Annalise. You were right all along. They tried to kill Joanie. We gave her a new life."

She knew it. "We?" Annalise's voice shook on the simple two-lettered word.

"WITSEC."

"I don't understand. How are you involved? Why didn't I know about it all this time?"

Milt leaned back in his chair. "I have a dual role. Norris Police Department is the one everyone sees. The United States Marshals Service is the one you don't."

"You're a Marshal?" Zach added.

"Mostly retired now. I monitor a few cases, keep an eye on a few Witness Protection members. Mostly in an advisory capacity now."

"Olivia is Joanie?" Annalise said.

"Yes. And she's in danger. She left me a note. They've found her, and she did what she had to do to protect Jonah and the kids." He folded his hands.

"You sending the samples in would raise too many red flags."

Clarity blossoming felt a lot like guilt. "I'm sorry, I didn't mean to—"

"Don't, Annalise. I should have been honest with you. I knew you'd figure it out." Milt smiled. "Your brilliant mind was bound to see the big picture."

A weight lifted from her heart. "How can we help now?"

"We have to find Olivia before they do."

"Who are they?" Zach leaned forward, propping his elbows on his knees. "And what do they want?"

"Revenge. Protection. Tie up loose ends. The possibilities are numerous. Olivia knows things about the Juarez Cartel she wishes she didn't." He chuckled mirthlessly. "I wish she didn't too."

"Where do we start?" Annalise said.

Milt sighed. "Open the letter, Zach."

"How did you—"

Annalise thought the same question Zach voiced.

"We need him." Milt rose.

"Who?" Zach whispered.

Milt put his hand on Zach's shoulder. "Your father."

Chapter Sixteen

If Zach hadn't been sitting already, he would have collapsed into the chair. As it was, he felt himself shrink a few inches, as if he was puddling into the fabric. "My what?"

"Open the envelope, Zach. Your father isn't who you think he is."

Before any of Milt's words could fully register, Annalise rose from the chair and exited the office. A few minutes later she returned and handed him the envelope.

The sound of him ripping the paper echoed loudly in the silent room.

Son,

Zach huffed. Really? Son?

Annalise patted his arm.

Let me start with I'm sorry. I know, no matter when you read this, it won't make it any better, but I did what I had to do to keep you and your mother safe. Believe it or not—

Not. Definitely not. Whatever was coming at the end of that sentence, Zach didn't believe it.

The two of you are my world. Always will be. As much as it hurts to leave, it would hurt worse seeing you suffer because of me.

But that's exactly what had happened. Suffering. For him and his mom, for more years than he cared to admit.

I am not who you think I am. My job is much too dangerous for me to continue being a presence in your life. I will be watching. Always. From a distance. I love you both.

Zach handed the letter to Annalise, who quickly read it and handed it back. He didn't take it from her. He couldn't move. No, this wasn't what he expected at all. No, the words didn't help dull any of the pain. In fact, the things he thought he'd dealt with years ago simply awakened and began to throb once more.

He looked to Milt, unsure what his expression was but knowing he must look like a lost puppy.

"Your father is CIA."

"How do you know this?" Annalise voiced the question Zach couldn't formulate.

"We were best friends."

What? How? When? Had he said any of those words aloud?

"I—I don't understand, Captain. I've known you for all this time, and you've been keeping two huge secrets from us." Annalise's voice shook as she spoke.

"I was sworn to secrecy." Milt shrugged, unapologetically. "But I need both of you on board now." He scratched a number onto a scrap of paper. "Call your father, Zach."

"No." Zach's veins burned as he fled from the room. Call his father? Milt couldn't be serious. There had to be hidden cameras somewhere. Or he was having a nightmare.

He stopped on the front walk and leaned onto the metal railing, begging it to lend him support and keep him upright.

Annalise's pearberry shampoo gave her away before she touched him.

"I can't just call my father. I haven't seen or spoken to him in—"

"I know. I don't understand what just happened either." She looped her arm around his left elbow and leaned against his shoulder. "Joanie is alive. Senator Marcum's case isn't really closed. The Juarez Cartel has migrated to East Tennessee. I'm pretty sure this is a bad movie."

Zach chuckled. "No joke."

"Or, yeah, a bad joke."

He wrapped his arm around her shoulder and pulled her to his side. He planted a kiss on the top of her head and closed his eyes. "I don't know what to do."

"Let's pray about it."

He bowed his head.

"Lord, please show us what to do about Zach's father. We want to find Olivia, of course, but this whole situation hurts. Give Zach clarity, and if he is meant to reach out to his father, help him be courageous and strong. Amen."

He kissed her head again. "Amen. Thank you."

"Do we have any other viable leads? Options? Tiny little rabbit trails of hunches to follow?"

"Nope. Not a one."

"Guess we'd better update Kirk, eh?"

"I think so."

Zach dialed and put Kirk on speaker phone. After Zach explained the situation, Kirk's response was simple. "Call your father. I know it's a sticky situation emotionally for you, man, and I'm sorry. But we have to do everything we can to find her."

Sticky emotional situation didn't begin to describe all the thoughts bouncing around like spear-studded foosballs in his mind.

"Thanks, Kirk. Please do not make any of this public information. Obviously, there is much more to this case than we initially thought," Annalise said.

"We had another case come in today. I'll handle it, and I'll keep Blu off your case as long as I can. You two run with this."

"Yes, sir." Annalise hit end on the phone in Zach's outstretched hand.

He was again frozen in place. The next call he made would change everything. And he wasn't ready.

Every muscle Milt had felt tight. He watched from the corner booth while Annalise and Zach whispered to each other a few tables over. Henry Leebow should be on his way. What was running through Zach's mind? Milt could imagine, and he felt badly about the situation, but what choice did he have? Olivia needed him, and he needed Henry.

The old-fashioned brass bell dinged as the front door swung open, and Henry stepped through. His hair was more silver, the wrinkles deeper, but his tall, muscular frame looked like it did when they were in their thirties. Henry nodded, barely perceptibly.

Milt gestured to Zach and Annalise. Once Henry was seated opposite them, Milt surveyed the periphery and then moved to join them. They really should've had the forethought to get a table instead of a cramped booth. But, oh well. He awkwardly shook hands with Henry. "Long time, no see."

"That was the plan."

Henry's voice sounded gravellier than Milt remembered. Had the man never stopped smoking cigarettes? "Good point. Well, we wouldn't have reached out had we not needed some serious help here."

Henry's small grin faded. "What kind of help, Milt?"

Captain Brooks glanced across the table. Zach's cheeks burned a brilliant red. Annalise's expression remained neutral, but Milt had a suspicion just barely. "Joanie's gone. You're the best at finding gone people."

Henry's mouth set into a hard line. "Tell me everything you know so far."

Annalise leaned in. "What about the case? If we solve the why, won't we find the who?"

She was smart. One of the reasons he'd fought so hard to bring her to Norris in the first place. "But, listen, Annalise. That 'case' doesn't exist anymore."

"How is that possible?"

Milt and Henry exchanged glances.

Henry cleared his throat. "We always suspected someone on the inside, within our own ranks, made it all slowly fade. At the time, evidence disappeared. We're lucky we even got a conviction against Senator Marcum."

Milt picked up where he left off. "And even then, it wouldn't have stuck had the person behind the mask not wanted it to."

"Do you have any ideas about who it might be?" Annalise asked.

"We each had our suspicions. Nothing that stuck." Milt took a sip of the fresh coffee the waitress had brought a moment ago.

Zach still sat rigidly with a blank expression on his face. When he spoke, Milt had to lean in to listen. "Are we really going to ignore the proverbial elephant?"

All movement at the table froze.

"We are going to sit here and pretend this man that I haven't seen in twenty years is a hero come to save the day?" He pinned them with a gaze, each in turn. "I won't do that." And disappeared out the diner's front door.

Milt couldn't say he blamed him.

Annalise emerged from the diner expecting Zach waiting on the sidewalk. She scanned the length of the street, but there was no trace of him. What now? A moment's indecision kept her lingering on the corner.

Where had Zach gone? She stopped, her breath pausing in her chest. And why was there someone in that parked car, watching her every move? She tucked her hands into her pockets and walked farther from the restaurant entrance, a shiver creeping up her spine. The car didn't follow. She ducked around the corner, pressed her back to the brick building, and whipped her phone out to text Captain Brooks. "We have a peeping Tom. Gray Buick."

She drew her weapon and peeked around the corner. The man's profile stood out black against the open space in the roomy old car. Still with no sign of Zach, she crossed the street casually and ducked into a clothing boutique's open doorway. In the front window, she rummaged through the front rack's selections of spring wear, but her focus was on the man in the car. From this angle she could see most of the license plate. She snapped a photo on her phone.

Come on, Captain Brooks, get out of there.

She eased down the sidewalk, sticking close to the building fronts to avoid the guy's passenger side mirror. But when she was within a couple feet, the car started, smothering her with a cloud of dark exhaust, and zipped away. Great.

She jogged back across the street and into the diner. Captain Brooks and Henry were gone. Apparently they were better at this whole slipping around unnoticed thing than she was.

A warm hand clamped onto her shoulder, making her jump and spin simultaneously.

"Geez, Zach, you nearly gave me a heart attack."

He grinned. "Sorry. Mind pointing that elsewhere?"

She lifted an eyebrow and, for a moment considered refusing until her heart could have a chance to regain its balance. "Where did you go?"

"For a walk. Needed to clear my head."

She tucked her weapon into its holster. "You see the gray Buick guy?"

He nodded. "Just as he was pulling away. What happened?"

"Nothing. He was watching the diner though. Let's get back to headquarters and run the plate."

"Deal."

"And we can talk about your dad on the way," Annalise said as she led the way out of the diner once more.

"No deal."

"Come on, Zach. We have to talk about this."

"Umm, no we don't."

She rolled her eyes.

"You didn't tell me when you were all worried about Dave last summer. We didn't talk about that."

"Yes, we did." She chuckled. "In fact, you practically pried it out of me. Remember?"

"Doesn't ring a bell."

She peered at him over the hood of his truck. "You don't, huh?"

"Not a single little chime." His mouth split into a wide grin. "Come on, nosy. Get in."

"Nosy!"

Zach disappeared into the cab.

"I am not nosy. I just care about you." She was talking to an empty street. "Oh, fine." Maybe she was a little nosy, but wasn't she allowed to be with him after all they'd been through together? He'd helped pull her through the ugliest months of her life recently, and she wanted to return the favor. Besides, if Milt thought they needed Henry's help, then they needed Henry's help. She expelled a massive sigh. It felt so good to be confident in Milt's motivations once more. She settled into the passenger seat and crossed her arms over her chest.

"Don't be mad at me."

"I'm not."

"Oh, yeah right."

"Let's just get back to the office. Maybe by then Milt and Henry will have some sort of plan formulated."

Zach growled.

"We need him, Zach. You don't have to like it."

"I don't."

"Olivia is priority number one. These guys ruined my and her life once already. Let's not let them do it again."

Chapter Seventeen

Someone's found me. She hadn't been fast enough. Olivia quickened her stride. She could see the bus station ahead, feel the pressure from the mystery person behind. Almost there. The gravity of her pursuer grew stronger, heavier, until a cold sweat trickled down her back. She glanced over her shoulder and a short burst of surprise fled from her lips. Too quiet to beckon for anyone's help, the sound disappeared beneath the roar of the Greyhounds.

She searched her memory for the face following her. Hispanic features with light eyes. Nothing set off any alarms in her head, but her heart pounded harder as the sound of his heavy breathing grew closer. Too close.

Olivia kicked into an awkward sprint, her backpack bouncing against her hips and back. If she could just make it to the safety of the open bus door, the driver would see her, would know she was in danger, and slam the door behind her, closing her assailant out.

A hand gripped her backpack strap and pulled, hard. Olivia spun to face him, raising her palm to the soft flesh beneath his chin.

The man's hand fell from her. He, obviously, hadn't expected her immediate reaction.

Olivia backed farther toward the bus.

But the man recovered quickly.

He lifted his shirt and withdrew a pistol from his sagging pants.

It had been so long since someone aimed a loaded gun at her chest. She froze and whipped her hands into the air.

"Atta girl. Now, come with me and no one gets hurt."

Had this goon taken his lines directly from a B-rated action movie? "Oh, yes. I believe you completely. I can tell by the look in your eye and the mannerism in which you carry yourself, you mean me no harm whatsoever."

He paused, a momentary eyebrow quirk lending confusion to the look on his face. "Just come with me, Ms. Sarcastic."

"Officer Sarcastic." She was pushing his patience and stalling for…what? She didn't have a plan here. But she knew if she followed him anywhere, she'd be dead before the next dawn.

The bus she'd been aiming for started, expelling a massive cloud of dark exhaust, covering her for a brief moment. She sprinted for the door and leaped through.

The driver looked up with wide eyes, glancing from her disheveled appearance to the man waiting behind her. "Ticket, ma'am?"

She handed it to him and ducked into the first seat behind the driver. "Please do not let him on the bus. In fact, call 9-1-1 if he even takes one step this direction."

"I understand, miss. Men shouldn't ever treat their women that way. You sure you don't want me to call it in now?"

She shook her head. "That won't be necessary. Let's just go, please."

"My pleasure."

As the bus pulled from the station, her heart rate slowed. But there was no guarantee the man wouldn't follow. She would have to duck off somewhere, disappear somehow. Again. And never reappear again.

"We've been watching the Juarez Cartel for years," Henry said from his perch atop the corner of Annalise's desk.

Zach waited in the corner, mere feet away from the interaction but miles away from the emotional ramifications. If he was cautious with his expectations, could he avoid letting his emotions concerning his father out of their box? He was certainly going to give it a good try.

"There are a lot of local names, little men in the big picture, but a lot of the people we need to speak with are still in Memphis." Milt continued, "I suppose we will split them up and begin questioning each and every one."

Zach snickered. "Yeah, that'll work."

Milt spun a tense gaze upon him. "You got a better idea?"

Only one thing kept recycling through his thought processes. And it was ugly and nasty and a whole host of other things, but it needed out of his mind. "Yeah, get rid of my paternal DNA donor and let Annalise and I help you."

Henry rose from the desk and, in a few long strides, stood nose-to-nose with Zach. "You have a problem, you say it directly to me. Do not disrespect me, son."

His heart leaped into his throat. He put his hands on his father's chest and shoved.

Henry took two steps backward and glared at him.

"You have no right to call me son." Zach gritted his teeth.

Annalise stepped between them, facing Zach with huge tears plaguing the corners of her eyes. "Zach, you're better than this."

He took a deep breath, finding calm in her features. "You know what, Annalise? You're right. I am better than," he gestured toward his father, "this. I would never leave my family. No matter what."

"Zachary Leebow, that isn't fair, and you know it. Go cool off and come back with your head clear and ready to do your job." Annalise nudged him toward the rear exit.

He hated when she used that tone with him. But it was effective, which is probably why he hated it so much.

In Annalise's oasis, he paced the length of the stone walkway, letting some of his anger out with each pounding step. Had he really just said those thoughts aloud? He searched his mind for remorse and found none. His father needed to hear how he felt, and Zach had only touched the surface. But saying it in the tone he'd just used probably wasn't his most mature moment.

Zach sank onto the bench next to a batch of feeders and hung his head between his hands. He had a job to do. He had a team of people counting on his dedication. *Lord, I need some help here. I have no idea to handle all of this. Give me patience and peace of mind until this case is over.*

After several silent moments with Him, Zach sighed deeply and reentered the office to find the group in the same position. "Give me and Annalise some names. We can go start the questions now."

Annalise smiled. "The first step is Michael Simpkins."

"Who's that?"

She lifted a printout. "The owner of the car at the restaurant. License plate search just matched him."

"Good." Milt reached for the paper. "Y'all start with him. Henry and I will start with an informant I used to know. The man's getting up in age now, but you never know. Maybe he'll remember something important."

Annalise drove them to Mr. Simpkins's sagging, street-side residence.

"Doesn't look like anyone's here."

Zach took in the details of each house lining the street on both sides. "Seems pretty quiet, but it is a workday."

"Let's take a quick peek around back. Maybe there's a downstairs garage or something."

"Following your lead, Special Agent Baker." He smiled, wishing he could feel it on the inside.

Fortunately, Mr. Simpkins's house occupied the corner. They made their way down the sidewalk, careful not to step over the presumed property line, until the rear of the house was fully in view.

"See anything?" he whispered.

"Tarp covering the vehicle in the far corner. The rear fender definitely looks like the Buick I saw at the restaurant."

"Want me to call it in?"

She nodded. "Let's wait in the car. Don't want to spook him if he's watching out the window."

Zach dialed as they walked back. He requested the search warrant. "Will be half an hour or so."

"Great." Annalise ducked inside her SUV.

He slipped into the passenger seat and cracked the window. "Pull into that parking spot a little farther down the street. We can keep an eye on the periphery of his house, in case he decides to sneak out the back."

She did as he instructed, and they settled into the seats, each watching a different area without needing to verbalize the plan. He loved that about working with Annalise. No matter what happened between them, no matter how out of whack his emotions or hers may be, the synchronization with which they operated never seemed to fail. Did it come simply from knowing each other most of their lives? From being a steady presence in each other's lives all these years? Or was there something more to their connection?

He hoped it was something more.

The unexpected thought paused his random musings. He hoped it was something more? Like what, exactly?

"Zach, look." Annalise touched his arm, and he jumped.

Thankfully, she didn't seem to notice.

A dark-haired man in jeans and a button-down shirt exited the front gate at the Simpkins's residence and started down the sidewalk in the opposite direction.

"We can't let him leave, warrant or no," Annalise said seconds before leaping from the driver's side.

He burst onto the street and into a sprint right behind her.

The man glanced over his shoulder and bolted down the hill toward the old St. Mary's Hospital building.

"Great!" Zach shouted to Annalise's now also running backside.

He ducked through two close-together houses and cut the corner short, rapidly checking the street both directions before regaining full speed. The man and Annalise disappeared into the parking garage ahead, but he had closed the gap fractionally.

Dialing the Knox County Police Department as he ran, he requested backup and then paused outside the entrance where he'd last seen Annalise. Across parking floor D, Annalise pursued the man through a doorway. If he remembered correctly, it led to a walkway that entered the main hospital tower. He raced to catch up. How was Annalise so much faster than him anyway?

At the exit from the garage, Zach pulled up short and peered around the corner. Annalise waited at the end of a short walkway, with the fugitive penned to the front of a locked door.

"Hands up, sir." She trained her weapon center mass and waited for the man to comply.

Instead, the man inched to his left, hopped the low, concrete wall and took off into the next section of the garage.

She spun. "Zach!" And motioned for him to round the corner and cut the man off.

As he turned to follow her instructions, she leapt over the wall and disappeared. When he made it to the next section of parking, neither of them was anywhere in sight.

The man's footsteps echoed from just ahead of her and out of sight around the curves of the parking garage as it rose to the higher levels. She pressed harder into her pursuit, her thighs burning as she ascended. Sunlight pierced the nearest to top level. She rounded the last turn and broke into dazzling light from a brilliant sunset.

It was too late to back up. She froze until her eyes could adjust. *Lord, I'm a sitting duck—*

A gunshot splintered the air.

Annalise dove to the rough concrete, her face scraping against the ground, and held her breath. A metal door slammed shut. She scrambled for the nearest car and crouched behind it. That was dumb. She could kick herself. Zach definitely would if he had witnessed her foible.

She drew a deep breath and peeked up through the windows of the car. There was no sign of

Michael Simpkins. Great. She called Zach. "I lost him."

"Are you okay? I heard a shot."

"Yeah, I'm fine."

"Annalise, seriously. You about gave me a heart attack. Hang on, I'm almost there."

She ended the call and stood erect, surveying the top of the garage as she did. She seemed completely alone with the empty cars. The door to the stairwell on the opposite side swung open. A woman with a briefcase and high heels exited. The door closed behind her, repeating the sound Annalise heard directly after the gunshot.

No doubt Michael was long gone.

Zach approached from her left and embraced her. He pulled back and stared into her eyes. "Are you sure you're okay?"

"I'm fine, Zach. Just mad that I lost Simpkins."

"Come on. Let's get back to the house before he can move the car while we are here."

Sirens echoed on the air.

"There's our backup, finally. I'll redirect them to the residence." He dialed, gave some quick commands, and hung up. "Come on. They'll meet us there."

They speed-walked back to the Simpkins residence. Three patrol cars, with their lights flashing, waited at the curb. The officers chatted in a huddle near the front gate. They grew silent as Annalise and Zach approached.

"We need to put an APB out on Michael Simpkins," Zach told the closest one.

Annalise grabbed her evidence kit from her SUV, made her way straight to the vehicle in the back, and yanked the tarp to the ground. It was definitely the car she'd identified at the restaurant. She slid on latex gloves and began processing the car, dusting it for prints, collecting the numerous pieces of trash, and inspecting the glove box and other compartments. She popped the trunk and peered inside.

Her breath caught.

Several long, brown hairs dotted the deep red carpet. She collected each of them and paused before spraying the luminol to check for blood. *Lord, please. I have a terrible feeling this test will be positive.* The sun setting half an hour ago provided the dark environment she needed for the fluorescent light to work. She sprayed the reactant into the trunk, sure to mist each surface, plugged in the light, and shone it into the trunk. Tiny blue dots glowed near the driver's side in a messy, haphazard drip pattern, as if one source of blood had been dragged across the surface. A nosebleed possibly? A small head wound? There would be no way of knowing until someone found and got answers from Simpkins.

"Zach!"

He stuck his head over the balcony porch railing, where he had been processing the kitchen just inside. "Yeah?"

"Got blood and hair. Escalate the status of the all-points bulletin."

Chapter Eighteen

Annalise slept fitfully for a few hours, but four a.m. found her in front of her glowing fireplace, with Millie at her side and a cup of hot chocolate, coffee mix. Though the lab would open in a few hours, it would take another few hours to process the evidence from the car and house.

Meanwhile, if Olivia was still on the move and not the victim from the trunk, she was slipping farther and farther away. So was Michael Simpkins. So was hope that they'd ever fully resolve the case that had led to such upheaval in her life.

And how did Jimmy Vern Buchanan manage to weasel his way out of punishment for so many of his crimes? She pulled up the email response she'd received from her inquiry after the trial.

It made no sense that a man who had fully confessed to kidnapping, murder, moonshining, aggravated assault, and a host of other smaller crimes would ever be eligible for parole. Yet, here was the proof. She could read the court summary a hundred times and it might never make sense. What exactly did he know about the Juarez cartel?

Though some of it had been redacted, it was clear enough Buchanan knew something huge, and was willing to put his life on the line in order to not have to put his life on the line. He'd agreed to share information in some big case, the name of which was blacked out—but which she'd already learned—in exchange for no death penalty. But it didn't stop there. After ten years in a minimum security prison, he would be eligible for parole. Unbelievable. How could he possibly know something that monumental?

A knock on the front door made Annalise slosh coffee onto her hand. Who on earth was there before dawn? She drew her weapon and eased to the front door, peeking through the eyehole. "Zach."

"I brought breakfast."

She opened the door. "What are you doing here?"

"Is that any way to greet your cinnamon crunch bagel?" He smiled.

"By all means, come in."

"I knew you'd be awake. I couldn't sleep either."

He handed her the bag and a large coffee cup. She peeked inside, inhaling the savory sweet aroma. "Aren't you eating?"

"Ate mine in the truck."

"Of course you did."

"No sign of Michael Simpkins. I just got off the phone with Milt."

"Lovely."

"They are coming over."

"They?" She knew he meant Henry, but she wasn't sure she wanted that tension in her living room.

"Yeah, I'll be good. I promise."

"You'd better. Are we going to talk about this mastodon any time soon?" Elephant status had passed hours and hours ago.

"We will. I'm still processing."

"I know, but I can help with that."

"I know, but I don't wanna."

"You sound like a spoiled teenager."

"So?" He elongated his whine and then sighed. "I'm really mad at him, Annalise. He had no right to let us believe…to let us wonder all these years."

"It wasn't your fault. Never was, Zach. Even if he had left for less valid reasons."

Zach slumped onto the couch and hung his head. "My head knows that. My heart, not so much."

She sat next to him and placed a reassuring hand on his shoulder. "You're an adult now. He is an adult. Surely the two of you can be adults about this situation."

"Maybe."

"I'm betting he feels just as badly, if not worse, about everything. Maybe, just maybe, you could give him a chance to show you the kind of man he really is?"

He shrugged her hand away. "I dunno if I can, Lise." He drew a ragged breath. "It hurts too much."

"I know." She understood emotional pain better than ever now, but she would never truly understand Zach's the way he did. Her parents were wonderful. Both of them.

Another knock echoed through the thick wooden door.

"I guess that must be them. You ready?"

He nodded, and Annalise let the haggard-looking men in.

Three hours later, with everyone hyped up on a zillion cups of coffee, they were no closer to figuring out where Olivia would have gone. Did the hair and blood in the trunk belong to her? The unspoken question floated in the air like an invisible mist, heavy and oppressive. Between that and the tension with Henry and Zach, the air in her living room became harder to breathe by the second. They were all four people of action, not of talking and waiting and wondering.

Henry excused himself to the restroom.

Annalise glanced at her watch. "I'll call the lab. They've been open an hour now. Maybe we will get a miracle."

She stepped into the kitchen to dial, but Zach stopped her. "How does Henry know where the restroom is?"

Annalise wrinkled her forehead. "I guess he just figured it was down the one hallway."

"There are five closed doors leading off the living room, Annalise. Why wouldn't he assume one of them was the guest bath?"

A weight sank in her stomach. "What are you getting at?"

"It's like he already knows the layout of your house."

Milt trusted Henry. Didn't that mean they could too?

"We don't know anything about him, do we?"

Annalise shook her head. "But Milt—"

Before she could finish her thought, Zach turned and stormed back into the living room. She hurried to catch up.

Zach stood at the end of the hallway, arms crossed over his chest, toe-to-toe with Henry. "How'd you know the bathroom was there?"

"Listen, son, it's my job to know what I'm walking into." Henry's tone bristled, but he didn't make a move to pass Zach.

"What does that mean?"

"I was here the other night, taking a look around the perimeter."

Zach's face flushed red. "You what?"

"I cannot be too careful in my line of work. You should understand that. Plus," his voice softened. "I wanted to see you."

"All you had to do was knock on the door."

"I…I wanted to."

Annalise's heart wanted to reach out to this man. Clearly, he had a tender side too. It was buried like Zach's often was, but it was there. "Listen, you two, discussion over. Henry, it was you that got Millie all in a tizzy the other night?"

Henry stepped around Zach and nodded.

"On the bright side, we have solved one mystery then. Let's get to work on the one that really matters."

She dialed the lab again and asked for an update.

"The hair fibers and blood match a deceased officer on file," the technician said.

Annalise's heart dropped into her toes. No, please no.

"Officer Joanie Greene, deceased in 2015."

Annalise thought she said thank you as she hung up, but she couldn't be sure. Olivia/Joanie had been in Michael Simpkins's vehicle. And not three years ago.

"What is it?" Milt asked.

"The DNA matches Olivia."

His face drained of all color. "It can't be. She's too smart, too good to…"

"We don't know anything for sure, sir. It was a minimal amount of blood." Annalise patted his shoulder.

"We must hurry. Her time is running out too quickly." Milt strode for the front door and disappeared through it, leaving it standing open to the morning sunlight.

The three of them looked at each other and then followed silently.

"Milt, where are you going?" Annalise called from behind him.

Where was he going, exactly? To Olivia. That's all he knew. But if that thug had her at some point, what were the chances she was still breathing?

Milt leaned over the hood, both hands planted flat on the fender and tried to draw a deep enough breath to make the dizziness abate. "I don't know." He could barely hear his whisper.

Annalise leaned across from him. "Okay, let's go find him."

He gave her a half-hearted smile. "Thanks, Special Agent Baker. Hop in." He'd known from the moment he hired Annalise, she'd be on his staff for only a short time. She had too much talent, too much potential to fade into the background of a sleepy town.

"Are you okay, sir?"

"No, not really."

"You must have known Joanie very well."

He could understand Annalise's curiosity, but he wasn't ready to share just yet. Yes, he'd known

Joanie well. He could still imagine her scrunched up little face the first time he'd held her. Still see her tears the first time she'd wrecked her bike.

"Turn left here, sir."

Milt shook himself from memories like faded photographs and did as she instructed. He glanced in the rearview and noticed Zach and Henry followed in separate vehicles. No surprise there.

"Maybe we missed something. Or maybe Simpkins came home." Annalise smiled.

"I appreciate your fake enthusiasm."

She chuckled. "I'm trying."

His steps felt lined with stones as he approached the front door. Swung it open and waited for his eyes to adjust to the darkness. His nose to adjust to the stale cigarettes and dirty laundry.

"Henry and Zach went around back." Annalise stepped through the threshold behind him.

A boot stuck out from behind the kitchen island. By the angle, he could tell it wasn't an empty one. His throat clenched even tighter as he spoke. "Annalise, look."

She slipped around him and approached the body. "It's Simpkins."

Great. He was their only connection to Olivia. And he was dead.

"Gunshot wound to the head. Close range."

Annalise's words sounded far away. Just like Olivia. Out there somewhere.

Never had he felt so useless, so lost.

Henry's strong grip clapped onto his shoulder. "Got a lead on Domingo, Milt."

"Where?"

"Local now. Must've followed the rest of them here."

At least they wouldn't be traveling to Memphis to speak with the man they'd considered second in command. Without proof, of course, and only in the privacy of Milt and Henry's personal communications. "All right, let's go."

"You two can handle this, right?"

Annalise nodded.

Zach remained a rigid rock in the corner.

Milt's mind wandered on the drive. Had it really only been five years since Memphis? It felt like a lifetime since he'd seen Olivia in person. He'd helped her disappear, redefine herself physically and on paper. She'd done the redefinition of her mental and emotional self by herself.

It had been the third most difficult decision he'd ever had to make, and yet easy since it was the only viable option to keep Olivia alive.

His first most difficult choice came when he left his first true love and their adorable little girl behind.

The second, when he chose divorce from a woman he loved but couldn't keep safe or happy. Walking away from her and their kids had almost killed him.

The third, sending Olivia into a new life utterly alone.

Milt sighed. Memory lane wasn't a pleasant stroll.

"You okay over there?" Henry glanced at him from the driver's seat.

"Yeah. Just worried."

"Yeah. I understand." He cleared his throat. "Domingo ain't changed much, if his last mug shot is accurate."

Milt chuckled. Domingo had been an ugly, tough nut to crack, sheltered as he was by the Juarez name and Marcum's influence over the town. Maybe things would be different now.

They found Domingo in the back room of a Mexican restaurant, surrounded by muscled men in suits. How cliché.

Henry stopped Milt with a hand on his arm. "Take a breath, partner."

Milt shook his hand free. "We haven't been partners in twenty years." He rushed the table, shoving it into Domingo's stomach. "We need to talk, *señor*."

The two men flanking Domingo jumped to their feet and drew flashy pistols from their waistbands.

Milt didn't flinch or make a move to draw his own weapon. He knew without looking that Henry covered him.

Domingo's face flushed purple, venom flashing in his eyes. "What do you want, Brooks?"

"I see you remember me. Good. Tell your boss he has something I want. And if I don't get it, the

Juarez family will not be able to continue to operate under our noses as it has been."

Domingo smirked. "What are you going to do about it, old man?"

Milt pushed the table tighter. "Keep grinning and you may find out. I got nothing to lose."

"Oh, really? Not Hannah and Kyle? Not Paul? How about that brother of his, Orrin?"

Milt didn't consciously choose his next move, but instinct and fear and fury propelled him over the table. He grabbed Domingo's shirt collar and dragged him over the wooden top. "Take me to her. Now. Or you really will find out what this old man can do."

"I'm sure I have no idea what you're talking about." Domingo smirked again.

Milt restrained himself from punching the man's front teeth out. But just barely.

Henry leaned in close to his ear. "These boys have itchy trigger fingers, Milt. It's time to go."

"I'm pretty sure I saw an unregistered firearm in Domingo's waistband. We'll be taking him in. Right, Henry?"

Domingo let out a frustrated sigh. "Shoulda known you'd find some ridiculous thing to drag me in for. Just like old days."

"Then you ought to know the drill. Maybe this time you'll be smarter and tell me what I want to know."

"Or what?"

Milt leaned in close. "I'll break your nose again." He smiled. "And this time, it will be on purpose."

Zach helped the medical examiner inspect Simpkins's body. The ME was a man of few words, communicating more through grunts and gestures. Zach interpreted the latest as lift the arm, which he did.

The doctor opened the dead man's curled fingers and showed Zach the palm.

"Annalise, write this down." He waited for her to get her pen and paper out, and then read the address aloud.

"This could be a huge break." Excitement laced her words.

"Or a pizza joint."

She shot him a look that said, "I'm not in the mood."

He grinned.

The ME glared at him.

He held back a chuckle. Wrong time to grin apparently. Or chuckle, no doubt. "Anything else, doc?"

"No, the medics and I can handle it from here. One bullet wound to the head, close range. I presume it was the cause of fatality, but I will need to perform a full autopsy to rule out other causes."

Zach resisted reminding the man he knew the drill. Instead, he whispered in Annalise's ear, "Let's go check out that address."

Annalise moved her head before he could pull away.

Her ear brushed his lips, hair tickled his cheek. He sucked in a breath as a wave of tingles swept over him.

She turned her face toward him, her wide eyes conveying a message he couldn't decipher. Her lips moved, but the words were lost to the pounding in his ears. What was happening to him? This was Annalise. His best friend. Just his best friend. Nothing more. He'd been arguing the same thing over and over again the last few weeks.

Annalise cocked her head and stared. "Did you hear me?"

"No." His voice sounded husky, even to him. He cleared his throat. "Sorry. What?"

"I said, I think we should check in with Milt and your father."

Instantly, his blood curdled. "Henry. Let's just call him Henry for now. Okay?"

She nodded. "I didn't mean—"

"I know." Zach spun on his heel and headed to the truck. He had to put some space between them before he did something stupid. Like kiss her.

"Look, Zach, I'm sorry." Annalise hurried after him.

How could he tell her what was bothering him? It was better to pretend it was because of his father, which wasn't really a lie either. Not exactly the problem at the moment, but definitely still a problem. "It's fine, Annalise." He tried to paste on a smile, but it felt weak. "Let's go see what was important enough to write on this guy's hand."

"Maybe he is just an idiot and couldn't remember someone's instructions."

He chuckled. "That is highly possible."

"Maybe I'm just an idiot too. I keep saying the wrong things. I'm sorry."

He stopped and wrapped her in a hug. "You are definitely not an idiot. You are amazing. You didn't say anything wrong. I reacted wrong." He kissed the top of her head, lingering a moment longer than usual. She smelled so good. She felt so good in his arms. He had to let go. Now.

"Zach?" Her voice, muffled against the front of his shirt, was what he needed to actually make his arms release her. "Are you sure you're okay?"

"Right as rain."

"Let's go find Olivia." She crossed her fingers. "I hope."

The phone's GPS led them to a green-shuttered home with a well-manicured lawn. Not what he expected. "Let's see if anyone's home."

Annalise knocked on the front door while he stood back and waited with his hand on his gun. The house looked innocent enough, inviting even. But something gave him a bad feeling in the pit of his stomach.

Footsteps sounded from the other side of the door.

A Hispanic man cracked the door. "We don't want whatever it is you're selling, *chica*."

Annalise put her foot against the door and whipped out her badge. "Special Agents Baker and Leebow. We have some questions."

The man's eyes widened, and the next instant he disappeared into the house. A gunshot burst the tranquility of the quaint neighborhood.

Zach drew his gun in one fluid motion and pushed Annalise away from the opening.

A second gunshot rang out, thudding into the back of the partially closed door.

"I'll circle around back," Annalise said.

He nodded.

After the third gunshot, from his position to the side of the open doorframe, he swung the door open and counted to ten. Either the man was waiting with a gun aimed at his heart when he stepped into the house or he'd run and Annalise would need backup when he made it to the back of the house. The second seemed like a scarier proposition, so Zach took a chance and peeked around the frame. No sign of the man.

The first few steps he expected to be ripped into by a flying bullet, but in fact there were no noises in the house whatsoever. Where was the guy? He cleared the den and dining room and rounded the corner to a tastefully decorated kitchen. Whose home was this?

Down the short hallway, he cleared a small bathroom and two bedrooms. Each of the beds showed signs someone had recently slept in them. He retraced his steps and found a door leading to what he presumed would be a basement. He cautiously made it halfway down.

"Don't come any closer, or I will kill her," the Hispanic man's voice sounded from somewhere below Zach.

"Kill who?" Not Annalise. Please not Annalise.

"Very funny. Isn't this why you're here?"

"I can't see you, so how am I supposed to know?" Zach took the last half of the stairway quickly and stood at the bottom facing the man.

A badly bruised woman with dried blood streaking her dark hair whimpered as the man tightened his grip on her neck.

Olivia Beck.

"Where is the other agent, the woman?" the man asked.

Zach shrugged. "Dunno."

"Let me leave or she dies."

"By all means, please. You may leave."

The man hesitated, a look of confusion passing over his features. "Put down your gun."

"Sure thing." Zach tossed it onto the mattress in the floor near Olivia's feet.

In the moment it took for the man to straighten his arm away from Olivia, Zach dove to the floor. The sound of the gun firing in the small space stabbed his eardrums. Zach rolled off the mattress, behind a thick wooden coffee table as the second shot split the air.

He watched the scene in slow motion through an opening in one end of the table.

The Hispanic man threw Olivia to the ground, where she crumpled into an unmoving heap. Then he sprinted for the stairs.

Zach had to help Annalise, but he couldn't leave Olivia either. He scrambled to Olivia's side and checked her pulse. It beat surprisingly strong against his fingertips. He gently removed the duct tape from her mouth. "I'll be right back."

Olivia's eyes fluttered. "Go. I'm fine."

"Don't go anywhere."

Olivia actually chuckled. "Right. I couldn't if I wanted to. Oh, wait. I do want to." She gave him a weak smile.

He grabbed his gun, took off up the stairs after the man, and slammed to a stop in the kitchen.

Annalise held the man at gunpoint. "Meet Carlos, Zach. He was just giving me his gun."

Carlos turned his head. Blood trickled from his nose and dripped onto his shirt.

"Carlos, I would do what the lady asks, if I were you."

He handed Annalise his gun and held his hands out for the cuffs. Carlos knew the routine obviously.

"I've got him, Annalise. Go say hi to Olivia."

Annalise's eyes widened, and her mouth dropped open. "You're kidding."

"Would I kid about something like this?"

"Yes."

"She's really here. I'll call an ambulance and backup."

"And Milt and Henry."

He nodded. "Go."

Chapter Nineteen

Annalise sprinted for the stairway and flew down them. She froze at the bottom and stared at her friend. Tears filled the corners of her eyes. "Joanie?"

Olivia turned toward her and smiled. "Annalise, hello. It's good to see you."

Annalise rushed to embrace her. "All this time, I thought you were dead."

"Ouch. Only halfway right now."

"Sorry." Annalise released her hold. "Zach's getting an ambulance."

Olivia's face paled. "No. I can't go to the hospital. They'll find me there."

"You need medical attention, Olivia."

"Help me up." Olivia struggled to rise to her feet. "Just get me out of here. I have to leave town.

They'll hurt my kids, Jonah…you have to help me, Annalise."

Her heart constricted. "Okay, just calm down. Everything's going to be fine. Zach has Carlos upstairs."

"Carlos means nothing to this organization. You don't understand. I finally know who's behind everything. They thought I knew before, but I didn't. Now I do and—"

The look on Olivia's face sent Annalise's heart into overdrive. It was clear she was terrified of the mystery man, whoever he was. "Who is it?"

Olivia shook her head. "I can't. We have to get out of here. Now."

"I can't let you—"

"If you don't help me, I'm disappearing again anyway, Annalise. I'm sorry to involve you, but—" Olivia took a step and collapsed against the wall. "I think they broke my foot."

Annalise rushed to help her friend. "Then you definitely need a hospital."

"I can't. I would rather die than put my family in more danger. These men will do anything to get to me. They can't find them."

"We can put your family in protective detail."

"Won't work."

"Why not? How could you possibly know that?" Annalise stared deeply into her friends large eyes. "He's law enforcement, isn't he?"

Olivia nodded.

"Okay, you're coming to my house."

"Thank you." Tears sprang to Olivia's eyes. "I owe you."

"I'm just glad you aren't dead."

Annalise helped her friend hop-hobble up the stairs. "Be right back." She left Olivia leaning against the couch and found Zach. "I'm taking Olivia home," she whispered. "Meet me there after you dump this yahoo. And don't call anyone just yet."

"Is that really the best idea?"

"It's the only one we've got right now." Annalise smiled. "Trust me."

"I always have, Lise. I'll be there as quickly as I can."

Annalise kept one eye on the road ahead and one on the rearview mirror. Olivia's physical discomfort was nothing compared to the anxious energy wafting from her side of the cab. "I'm calling Milt. He has been worried sick."

"You can't."

What? She had to call him. "I—"

"Every single person who knows about me is in danger already. If Milt knows you've found me, it puts an even bigger target on his back. Please, not yet."

Olivia's trembling voice made Annalise pause her dialing finger. "Okay."

"Look, I need some bandage supplies, maybe a walking boot from Walgreens or something. As soon as I doctor myself up, I'll be out of your hair."

"Joan—Olivia, that isn't at all what I worry about. I want to help, I just don't know how."

Olivia grunted. "Neither do I."

Milt yanked Domingo from the truck by his collar. He'd managed to get the man to at least stop ranting and raving about unlawful arrests and racist white cops.

Henry joined them at the front of the truck, where Milt pressed Domingo's chest against the hood and tried to cool his roaring temper. If he didn't get himself under control, he was liable to do more than break Domingo's nose.

"I'll scope things out." Henry disappeared inside the empty building and returned moments later. "All clear."

"This ain't the precinct, Brooks." Domingo shifted and met Milt's gaze.

"Look how smart you've become in your old age, Dom."

"I ain't Italian."

Milt chuckled. "No, you certainly aren't. I'd be willing to bet you'd know how to treat a lady if you were."

"What lady?"

Milt punched Domingo's stomach, hard.

While Domingo doubled over to catch his breath, Milt pulled him into the abandoned store and pulled what was left of the blinds.

"Things are gonna go a little different this time around, Dom." Milt sat Domingo in a chair. "See, this time I have nothing to lose. Because you already have something precious to me."

For the first time, Domingo's crooked, cocky smile faded. "I don't know what you're talking about."

"I don't believe you." Milt bound Domingo's feet to the chair legs and his hands behind his back. "My friend here has a lot of experience in this particular domain. If you don't talk now, I'll leave you to him."

Domingo's face paled. "I don't know nothing. You know I'm not in charge. Come on, Brooks."

"Not the answer I was looking for." He clicked his tongue. "Last chance, Dom. Where is she?"

"I don't know. I swear."

"Okay, *amigo*." He waved Henry over. "You know the drill." Milt's conscience prickled, but he shoved it aside. If this pond scum wouldn't tell him where his Olivia was, he was bringing Henry's methods down on his own shoulders.

Milt sneaked out the front door and leaned against the wall in front of the building. How many years had it been since Henry had been officially government sanctioned to retrieve information by whatever means necessary? Had Henry secretly been pleased when Zach came under Milt's watch? He knew Henry had kept an eye on his family from a distance, but maybe it helped to know his excomrade was keeping an eye on his son. Milt shrugged.

Had Henry extracted Olivia's location from Domingo yet? He glanced at his watch. It had only been three minutes. Ugh.

At some point, he was going to have to apologize to Annalise and Zach for withholding the full truth from them. Though it had been in their best interest to not get involved, Annalise especially, it weighed heavily on his mind. He'd come to care deeply for them both, and there was no place for dishonesty in relationships.

He'd learned that the hard way when he and his ex-wife divorced and took the kids. Hard to believe it'd been a decade ago already.

Ten minutes and counting. Good. Letting his thoughts wander was killing time like he'd hoped.

A gunshot splintered the air.

Milt jumped from the wall and raced inside.

Domingo's prostrate form lay close to the rear exit. A pool of blood was spreading rapidly around him.

"What happened?"

"Tried to escape." Henry tucked his gun into his waistband.

"How? I tied him hand and foot."

"He had a knife tucked into his back pocket. Sawed himself free. When I went to the kitchen for…supplies, I came back and he was sprinting for the door."

How did I miss that? Milt sighed. "Did he at least tell you where she is?"

Henry shook his head.

Milt spun and punched the closest wall. Shattering pain shot through his knuckles. Their best lead was dead, and he'd broken his hand. Fantastic.

Chapter Twenty

Zach tried Annalise's front door and found it locked for the first time he could ever remember. He knocked on the heavy door.

Footsteps approached from within, the curtain at the window to the left of the door pulled back, and then Annalise swung open the door. "Hey. I'm glad you're here."

"Where is she?"

"Resting in my room. She needs a doctor but refuses to let me call or take her anywhere."

"She's been through a lot."

"Simpkins is dead. Carlos is in jail now, right?"

Zach nodded.

"I want to call Milt and check in, but she made me swear not to."

"Interesting. As much as Milt cares about her disappearance, I would think she'd want him here."

"Me too. But she claims if she lets him know, it will only put him in more danger."

Zach scrunched his brow.

"I tend to believe her. This gang is ruthless. They burned my house down, killed numerous people in Memphis, and have seemingly followed Olivia across an entire state just to clean up loose ends."

"We'd be better served to play it safe. I agree with Olivia."

"Me too. But it's hard not telling Milt. And Henry."

"Not a problem for me, shutting Henry out." Zach chuckled.

"Yeah, I suppose not." Annalise returned his smile. "Come on, I'll fix you lunch. I'll bet you're hungry."

"Starved."

"I wouldn't have expected less."

He seated himself across the counter from her and watched as she deftly prepared lunch for them. He rather enjoyed seeing her in the kitchen, and for a moment he could imagine her in the role of housewife again very easily. His wife. He grinned.

She turned and caught him staring. "What?"

"Nothin'."

"I don't believe you, but I'm willing to let it pass." She set a plate in front of him. "Eat up."

"Thank you."

"Why didn't they just kill her as soon as they found her?"

"Good question."

"She knows something."

"Or they think she does."

Annalise's fork paused midair. "She said the leader was law enforcement."

His stomach knotted. "That brings a new level of complication to the situation. Do you believe her?"

"I do."

"Then it makes sense she is urging us to be even more cautious than ever."

"Who are you?"

Zach raised his gaze to find a dark-haired woman with her arms crossed over her chest glaring at him. "Olivia, I presume." He rose to shake her hand. "I'm Annalise's partner, Special Agent Zach Leebow."

She scowled. "I told you no one else, Annalise."

"Zach doesn't count. If I'm involved, he's involved."

Zach's chest swelled. "We're a team. Always have been, always will be. Besides, I was at the house too. Already saw you." He patted Annalise's back as he returned to his seat. "I'm here to help."

Olivia uncrossed her arms. "Fine. But, seriously, we have to get away from here. I do anyway."

"You need rest," Annalise said.

He couldn't agree more, but they didn't need another dog in this fight. "I know a doctor we can trust. Let me call her."

Annalise met his gaze. "Good idea. Why didn't I think of that?"

"Are you two listening to me at all?" Olivia joined them at the counter.

"You need a doctor. And you need our help." Annalise fixed her a plate while she talked. "If you're right, we're in danger just having you here. But if we don't get you patched up, there's no way you can run from these guys."

"Or stand and fight." He gestured to the foot she'd hobbled in on and now had propped against another stool. "Your foot looks bad."

Olivia ducked her chin. "It hurts, but I can manage. At least until this is over."

"The doctor is coming. Deal with it." Zach texted his mom. "We need some medical assistance. Annalise's house. A friend. Possible broken foot."

She answered almost immediately. "Go to the hospital."

"It's complicated, Mom. Can you please come? Be careful, and watch your back."

"Okay. Be there in a half-hour."

"Thanks." Zach smiled. "There. She is on her way."

"You two are even more stubborn than me." Olivia grinned. "Someone should check the periphery."

"I got it." Zach swallowed the last bite of his BLT and a swig of soda. "Be back in a jiffy."

The afternoon sun warmed him through his long sleeves, making him push them toward his elbows and unbutton the top couple. Summer would be here soon. Would it bring as many cases? He had no doubt SMIF would be busy. A year ago, he only wished for an opportunity such as this. Now it was reality and, yet, something was still missing.

Annalise's smile flashed to mind. Her lips…

He stopped his daydream before it could wind any farther along its dangerous trail.

Zach circled the house. On the first pass, checking the near proximity, checking windows and doors, and on the second pass scanning the forest edge surrounding her cabin. Nothing seemed out of place. As he rounded the front again, his mother pulled in. He gave her a quick hug. "Can I carry anything for you?"

"You weren't very specific, son, so I have a huge bagful of supplies in the trunk. Can you grab it?"

He kissed her head. "Of course. Thanks, Mom."

Zach waited near the door while his mom examined Olivia on the couch in the living room. Something about having the two most important women in his life in one room, with the threat of the Juarez Cartel hovering in the air like a silent specter, made his skin extra-special tingly.

"I can't be sure without an x-ray, but you have the telltale purple line, swelling, and pain on palpation. Are you sure you won't go to the hospital?" his mom questioned Olivia.

She shook her head. "I can't."

"Okay, then, to be on the safest side possible given the circumstances, I am putting you in a walking boot. Don't take it off. I can't promise you don't need surgery to set bones, young lady."

Annalise took Olivia's hand. "Are you sure about this, Joan—Oliv…Are you sure?"

"Yes."

"I'm also giving you a prescription for antibiotics. Some of your lacerations are fairly deep." His mom examined Olivia's head. "Tender here?"

Olivia nodded.

"Dizziness? Fuzzy thoughts? Sleepiness?"

"Yes, yes, yes."

His mom pulled back and, with one hand on each of Olivia's shoulders, held her at arm's length. "What happened to you?"

Olivia's face flushed. "Would you believe me if I told you I was in a car accident?"

"No, but obviously you aren't going to tell me what happened. I presume you're in some kind of trouble." She glanced at Zach.

He smiled.

"But, you're in good hands." His mom looked at Annalise. "With both of these hooligans."

"Okay, Mom. If that's all, we've got to get you out of—"

Millie leaped to her feet. Her wild bark filled the entire inside of the cabin. She ran from her position at the fireplace to the front door and growled, a low rumble that made the hair on the back of Zach's neck stand up.

"No…we didn't…we weren't fast enough." Olivia struggled to her feet, even more awkward with the large fracture boot on her foot.

"Mom, get to the hall bath. Now. Do not open the door, no matter what you hear." Zach aimed his mother toward the hallway.

"But—"

"Mom, I mean it. Stay there." Zach hated making his mom's eyes look that way, so wide and filled with fear, but he needed her to know how serious he was. He gently pushed her into the bathroom and met her glance. "Stay. Put." Shutting the door, he drew his weapon and returned to the living room. He nodded at Annalise, who was already waiting by the door.

Annalise pulled the door open and peeked out. "I don't see anyb—"

A fusillade of bullets slammed into the front of the house. Zach yanked Annalise back into the house and slammed the door. The sounds of the automatic weapon spouting off so many rounds at once deafened him. "Did you see any sign of someone out there at all?" he shouted.

"No! They must have been behind my SUV."

Millie's frantic barking filled what little empty sound space was left.

"How many rounds have you got?"

"Two clips. You?"

"Same."

"I've got the .410 in the bedroom with a few shells."

The roar subsided.

Millie calmed to a low growl.

He and Annalise returned fire through the curtained front windows, now missing most of the glass. He caught movement near Annalise's SUV and aimed low, hoping to hit the man's feet. The bullets thudded into the gravel, spraying rocks into the undercarriage.

Annalise had a second man ducking behind his mother's car.

Were there truly only two? Or did more men wait for them to make a run for it out the side door?

He glanced at Olivia. Her pale face and tremoring told him she was in no condition to fight, though she was bravely trying to hold her position at the side door with Annalise's extra handgun. She was certainly in no condition to run.

They had to get out of here before they were surrounded and infiltrated. Whoever was out front had their only mode of transportation blocked off. "We need backup."

"But we can't, Zach." Annalise motioned toward Olivia.

"I know." He leaned in close. "Text Milt. Tell him to come on foot. Alone. And to let us know when he is close."

"What do you have in mind?"

Zach grinned, though he didn't feel any jubilation whatsoever. "Something stupid."

"Imagine that."

A second round of gunfire opened on Annalise's beautiful cabin. He and Annalise both ducked behind the thick front door. What was left of the windows popped and crashed to the ground, sending Mille into another furious barking round.

Annalise drew her beloved pet to her and tried to calm her. "Milt says he was already on his way. ETA five minutes."

"Good. I'll buy us some time. You still have all those fireworks in the kitchen?"

She hesitated. "Yeah."

"Good thing it rained us out on New Year's, eh?"

"I guess so."

"Watch Olivia, keep your eyes peeled, but don't shoot me. Okay?"

She chuckled. "I only have one clip left. Don't do anything too stupid."

That's what he was aiming for. He kissed her forehead. "Be right back."

Chapter Twenty-One

Milt repeated the text from Annalise over and over in his head as he slowly climbed the steep incline of her driveway. "Shots fired. Don't call anyone. Come in on foot. Two men out front. Be on the lookout for more."

Why was someone shooting at Annalise's home? And, more importantly, why couldn't he call in backup? Had Annalise learned something more about the Juarez Cartel?

At the last bend before her cabin came into view, Milt ducked behind a tree. Paused. And attempted to catch his breath. He was too out of shape for this.

Explosions of various intensities broke the air from the direction of Annalise's house. He jumped, and his mind reeled into get-moving mode. More gunshots? Colors burst overhead, sizzling as the fireworks' sparks settled over the treetops. What in the world?

Careful to stay close to the forest-bordered edge of Annalise's driveway, Milt tiptoed closer. The cabin came into view first and then the vehicles parked out front. As promised by text, two armed men crouched behind the SUV. Their faces turned toward the firework display overhead gave Milt just enough distraction to creep closer.

"Hands up."

The first man spun and lowered his gun's aim toward Milt's chest.

Milt squeezed the trigger, and the man dropped. He swung his gun toward the second. "Don't make me shoot you too."

He hesitated for a moment and then aimed for Milt.

Milt's second bullet found its mark and this man, too, fell to the gravel. He whipped his phone out to dial 9-1-1 as he sprinted to check on the men.

"Stop, Milt!" Annalise's cry came from the front porch.

He looked up and found Annalise and Zach sprinting toward him. He put the phone away. "They're dead."

Annalise hugged him. "We have to get out of here." She tossed the keys to Zach. "Start the SUV. I'll grab them."

"Grab who?" Milt's brow wrinkled.

"It's a long story. One we will tell on the road."

"I don't understand. What is going on?"

"No time, Milt. Get in."

He rounded the vehicle and opened the passenger door, but froze as his gaze found the woman hobbling down the front stairs. "Olivia!"

He rushed to embrace her. "You're alive." Tears clouded his vision. "Thank you, God."

She looked up into his eyes and smiled. "Hi, Dad."

Dad? Had Annalise heard Olivia correctly? As much as she longed to hear the details, they'd have to talk about it later. "Come on, guys, we've gotta go."

Annalise ushered Milt, Olivia, and Lorraine to the SUV and then tucked Millie into the back. The sight of the men lying in her driveway made her stomach knot. Leaving them like discarded trash was so very wrong. She slid into the seat behind Zach, next to Olivia and Milt.

Zach met her gaze in the rearview. "When we're on the road, we'll call it in."

She sighed and nodded. "Thanks." Every cell in her body trembled as she settled into the seat. Had they really just experienced a full-on shootout at her home? The place she was supposed to feel safe. She chuckled mirthlessly. None of her homes had felt safe in the end. The first one burned by the Juarez Cartel. The second one where Dave deceived her for far too long. The third one turned into Swiss cheese by the Juarez Cartel. Lovely.

"I hate to state the obvious, but where are we going?" Milt asked.

"I don't really have a plan here," Zach replied.

"How about the safe house? The first one?" Olivia directed her thoughts toward Milt.

"Safe house?" Annalise scrunched her brow.

"When I disappeared from Memphis, we had a safe house outside of Nashville. Near Fall Creek Falls."

"It's worth a shot," Milt said.

"All right. Tell me how to get there." Zach put his blinker on to head toward the interstate. "After I drop my mom off."

"Don't you think they will figure out where she lives? We just left her car there with two bodies." Annalise sighed. "And a gazillion bullet holes in my house."

"Good point."

She knew Zach worried his mother would be even more in harm's way if they brought her along.

"What about Paul, Milt?" Zach asked.

"He could use some supervision since it looks like I may be away a while."

"Mom, what do you say? Wanna hang out with a teenager in a quaint town for a couple days?"

"I don't know, Zach."

"Please, it would make me feel so much better knowing you're somewhere safe."

Annalise leaned forward and placed her arm on Lorraine's shoulder. "Milt can have an officer stationed at his home. And you know Zach isn't going to let this go until you give in."

Lorraine sighed. "Oh, all right. Let me get some essentials."

"You made the right decision, ma'am," Olivia added. "These men are ruthless." She paused. "And well connected."

The trip to Lorraine's house went smoothly. Annalise helped her pack the items she needed and they zipped north on seventy-five to drop her at Milt's house. A police cruiser parked sideways in Milt's driveway gave Annalise some hesitation.

Zach voiced their consensus of concerns. "Milt, you expecting anyone?"

He shook his head.

"Stay here, Mom."

Zach, Annalise, and Milt exited the SUV with their weapons drawn. As they approached the front steps, an officer emerged and instantly lifted his hands.

"Hey, what's up, Captain?"

"Freddy, you about gave me a heart attack." Milt holstered his gun. "Is something wrong?"

"Nah, brought you a guest."

"What?"

"Orrin Martin. He was released on parole today. Said he wanted to see his little brother."

Annalise tucked her weapon into her belt holster and noticed Zach did the same. It was hard to read the expression on Milt's face. They followed him inside.

Paul sat on the couch facing his older brother.

"Did you know about this, son?" Milt asked.

"No, sir."

"He ain't your son," Orrin added.

"This is my house, young man. You want to tell me why you're here?"

Orrin's face flushed. "I came to see my baby brother." He smiled and punched his brother's leg playfully.

Paul didn't move, didn't change the stony expression on his face.

"Captain, this is terrible timing," Annalise said, "but we really ought to hurry. Don't you think?"

"You can't stay here, Orrin. I'm sorry. Like Annalise said, the timing is terrible. We can sort this all out when I get back."

Zach eased out the door. "I'll wait with the ladies."

"When you get back?" Paul raised his gaze to Milt's. "You're leaving?"

Milt sat next to Paul on the couch. "I've got a family emergency to deal with."

The pained look on Paul's face tugged at Annalise's heartstrings.

"Now, not that you're not family now, Paul. 'Cause you are." Milt patted Paul's shoulder. "It's safer if you aren't involved. Trust me?"

Watching the quiet moment between them made Annalise realize just how close these two had grown over the past six months. Though Paul was about to turn eighteen, Milt had mentioned adopting him. "So the boy will have a real family," he'd said.

"You remember Officer Leebow that was just in here?"

Paul nodded.

"His mother will be staying with you for a couple days."

"Aw, come on. I don't need a babysitter."

"No, but she needs a place to stay. I expect you to treat her with respect, son."

"Yes, sir."

"And Millie too?" Annalise asked.

"Yes, that's fine." Milt smiled and then turned his attention to Orrin. "As for you, we'll drop you at the hotel on the way out of town. I expect you to be there when I return."

Annalise recognized the tone in Milt's voice. He meant business.

Orrin's eyes widened. He nodded. "Yes, sir."

"Good. Annalise, get Lorraine and her things, please."

"Yes, sir." She hurried back outside. They needed to put distance between the Juarez Cartel and Olivia Beck. As soon as possible.

Chapter Twenty-Two

Annalise waited on the front porch of a modest, inconspicuous home, while Milt entered the code into the automatic door lock.

"Always the current president's birth year."

Annalise smiled. Interesting choice but easy enough for many agents to remember, even one like Milt who hadn't been an active agent in years. "How long has this been a safe house?"

"Twenty years or more."

She glanced over her shoulder toward the driveway.

Zach helped Olivia from the SUV.

She held up a hand to ask them to wait. She and Milt entered the cabin to clear it. "And no one has figured it out yet?"

"Hasn't been used very much that I know of. Plus its ownership is buried in mounds of paperwork and shell corporations."

"On paper whose is it?"

"A doctor turned businessman with five homes. This is his summer getaway."

"All fictional?"

"Of course." Milt checked the last window for anything suspicious. "Though if anyone can figure it out, it will be the Juarez Cartel. They always know everything."

Annalise glanced out the door. Zach and Olivia still waited for word to come in, chatting quietly by the driveway. She dropped her voice. "Olivia said she knew who the inside officer is."

Milt's eyes grew wide. "I don't know if that's good or bad news."

"I know."

"If he knows she knows, her chances of surviving went from very little to even worse."

Annalise nodded. "She saw him. He knows."

Milt leaned on the couch for support. "We have to stop them before they—"

"She has to know something, Milt. Or she would be dead already."

"Like what?"

The snap in his voice was like the sting of a whip. "I'm not implying anything bad, sir."

He sighed.

"But you know how ruthless they are."

"You're right. Let's get them in here where it's marginally safer."

Zach's eyes snapped open. It wasn't his watch, but something triggered his spidey-senses. He chuckled. Annalise would get the joke, if she were living in his brain and could hear his thoughts.

The house seemed quiet. He knew Milt was sitting in the rocking chair on the front porch, precisely where they'd all left him—he glanced at his watch—two hours ago. It was almost Annalise's turn, then it would be his. He needed to sleep while he could. The last days had been exhausting, but his mind didn't seem very sleepy anymore.

Too bad his fath—Henry wasn't here. It would give them another set of eyes.

The thought made him pause. Interesting. He hadn't expected to want Henry involved at any point during this whole ordeal. *Lord, could You please give me some wisdom here? I know what I should do, what You tell us to do, but I'm not sure I can. Forgiveness doesn't seem possible in this case.*

He rolled over, snuggled under the covers, and closed his eyes. But it was too late. His mind was awake. He flipped the covers off and got dressed.

Milt was in the almost exact same position on the front porch. With a rifle across his lap from a stash of weapons and ammunition in the cabin and a Thermos of coffee, he looked like a television character waiting for a dating daughter to arrive. "Couldn't sleep, eh?"

Zach slipped into the rocker next to him. "I got about an hour."

The front door swung open and Annalise stuck her head out. "Everything okay?"

"Can't sleep."

She stepped fully through the door and pulled the blanket around her shoulders closer. "Me neither."

"Come join us." Milt filled an extra mug and extended it to her.

"What happened to your hand, sir?' Annalise asked as she sank onto the swing and yawned.

"Long story."

Zach quirked an eyebrow. "Sounds intriguing."

"Involves a potential witness and a wall. Didn't end well." Milt chuckled mirthlessly.

Zach's gaze returned to Annalise, with her hair mussed and her eyes rimmed in dark circles. A sight he'd seen before. But, somehow, this time it took his breath. What would it be like to witness this version of Annalise every morning? For the umpteenth time he had the same thought. Dave was an idiot to throw her away.

She smiled at him, and he had trouble returning the gesture.

He tore his gaze from her to take in the details of the lawn. It was much safer. The full moon was in their favor, at least. A large yard stretched down a gentle slope toward a thick forest encircling the entire property. Beyond the lush layer of trees, the road waited. An occasional car meandered by, even at this hour, its headlights flashing like tiny white orbs between the trunks. As long as none of them stopped. Not even Kirk knew their location, and that needed to be the case, but it sure made him feel vulnerable. If they needed help, no one would come. They were truly on their own.

"Well, if you young'uns have this covered, I think I'll turn in." Milt yawned.

"After all this coffee?" Annalise teased.

"I can sleep through anything, kid."

Zach noted the blush on her cheeks. She looked up to this man. Him calling her "kid" was a compliment.

"Before you go, you've got to satiate our curiosity, Milt."

Milt chuckled. "Yes, Annalise, Olivia is my daughter."

Zach's eyebrows shot up. Daughter? How?

"My first marriage. I was young, very young, and in love. We had a daughter, and then I chose to walk away. My ex-wife took Joanie—Olivia—with her. I was twenty-two. It was safer."

"Wow, sir. I had no idea."

Zach didn't either.

"My career plan was clear. I let them go because I knew my life would be dangerous soon." Milt's eyes darted to meet Zach's.

Henry had seemingly done the same thing. Maybe, just maybe Zach could look at it as valor rather than abandonment. Someday. *Maybe soon, Lord?*

"Thankfully, Olivia's mom kept me in the loop as much as possible. I saw her frequently for a lot of years."

Zach grimaced. Milt had missed his daughter's life too.

"I know what you're thinking, Zach." Milt spoke without looking at him. "But you won't understand until you have children of your own. You'd do anything to protect them."

Zach gritted his teeth. Something was changing inside him. Was it going to be good for him or bad?

"Your father loved you, still loves you. You may never forgive him, but I encourage you to. Olivia and I haven't seen each other face to face in years, but we have a great relationship."

"I don't think—" He couldn't finish the thought. It wasn't true. He wanted to keep his heart hardened against his father forever. It was easier. It didn't hurt as much as possibly letting the man in and then being let down again. But instantaneously realization set in. Zach wanted to forgive him. Wanted to know what it was like to have his dad in his life.

Annalise raised her eyebrows and pierced him with a serious stare. And then smiled.

She knew what he was thinking.

"All right, kids. One of you really should get some sleep, if you can. I'll see you at dawn. We'll make a plan then."

"Yes, sir," Annalise answered for both of them. Once Milt had entered the house and shut the door, she turned to him. "I'm proud of you, Zach."

"I didn't...I haven't..."

"You will. And I'm proud of you."

His heart warmed, as did his stomach and chest and the rest of him. Oh, good. More tingles. "Want to do a perimeter check with me?" He leaped to his feet.

Annalise jumped. "Sure."

They circled the house slowly, silently. He kept his eyes peeled for anything unusual. *Thanks for the moonlight, Lord. It's perfect timing for this kind of thing.*

Back in the front yard, he pulled to a stop and gazed up at the clear sky, filled with stars and bright white light. It was beautiful.

Annalise leaned her head on his shoulder. "Full moon is kind of a lonely thing, don't you think?"

"I guess so, yeah."

"I always thought I'd always have someone to stand in the moonlight with me, you know?"

Zach drew a deep breath and dipped his chin. His voice dropped to a husky whisper he couldn't change if he tried. "I'm standing here with you, Lise."

She raised her head and looked up at him, her eyes as big as the moon shining above. Her eyebrows wrinkled and a look of something new flitted briefly across her eyes. "Yes, you are."

It took every ounce of strength in every fiber of his being for him not to lean into her lips and taste them. Could she read in his eyes the passion he felt rising? The love that slammed into him like a March wind?

She cleared her throat and took a step back. "Everything seems clear. I think I'll catch a couple more hours, if you are good to stay awake?"

He nodded because no words would pass the barrier of his pulsating emotions.

Chapter Twenty-Three

Annalise hurried into the safe house, her heart pounding in her ears. She closed the door behind her and leaned against it. That was close. She'd felt certain Zach was about to kiss her, and that she would wholeheartedly return said kiss. And that couldn't happen.

Could it?

She shook her head. No, absolutely not. Unless maybe…

Ugh. What was she doing? What was she thinking? She pressed her hand to her chest. She just had to calm the racing of her heart and her thoughts would get back on track. And get a few more hours of sleep.

Tomorrow they'd have to figure out their next move. *Lord, please keep us all safe. We've got*

Olivia, and I am so thankful. But she needs recovery time where she doesn't have to run from anyone and no bullets are flying at her. Thank you.

Annalise made her way to the kitchen and prepared a cup of peach tea she found in the pantry. Who kept this place stocked? How had they kept it a secret all these years?

She had so many more questions, most of which would probably never have answers. She plopped into a kitchen chair and wrapped her hands around the warm mug. The ones they had to focus on were not about safe houses and tea. The Juarez Cartel had played havoc in too many people's lives for too long. Not only with their revenge tactics but the drugs they pedaled onto the streets daily.

So much for more sleep. It seemed her brain was as restless as her heart tonight. She might as well get dressed and relieve Zach. Or at least keep him company.

A few moments later, in a new pair of jeans and a sweatshirt they'd bought at a Wal-Mart in Cookeville on the way in, Annalise stepped into the moist, cool early morning air. Zach wasn't in the rocking chair where she'd expected to find him. She sat on the swing and waited for him to finish his perimeter rounds.

And waited.

And waited.

What was taking him so long? Chills crept up her arms, making the hairs on the back of her neck tingle. Something wasn't right.

She drew her gun and rose slowly from the swing to avoid making the chains creak. The moon rested farther toward the western horizon but still provided enough light to see clearly. She hugged the corner of the house as she swung around. And gasped. "Zach?" she whispered.

The form on the ground didn't move. Inching closer, she attempted to suppress the galloping in her chest. "Zach?"

There was still no movement.

She dropped to one knee and shook him. "Zach, what happened?"

He moaned. His eyes fluttered open. "My head."

Annalise rotated his face from her to find a nasty gash on the back of his skull. Blood oozed from it, coating his light hair. Nausea and nerves overtook her stomach. Someone else was here. "We have to get you up."

"Someone hit me."

His slurred words warned her he may have a concussion. "Can you sit up?"

He struggled to rise and patted his side. "My gun. It's gone."

"Come on, Zach. We have to move," her hoarse whisper echoed so loud in the otherwise quiet side yard. "Now."

She got him to his feet, looped his arm around her shoulder, and began pulling him toward the front porch. They had to wake the others and formulate a defen—

Why did she suddenly get a strong whiff of smoke?

"I'm dizzy, Annalise." Zach staggered. "So dizzy."

"Here." She leaned him against the side of the house. "Hang on." She peeked around the corner. The porch was clear. If she could reach just a little farther... Her fingers brushed against the butt of the rifle lying across the nearest rocking chair. She stretched even farther, feeling the pull through her biceps into her back, and grabbed the piece she could reach. She slid it slowly into her arms.

"Take this." She put the gun in Zach's trembling hands. "Just don't shoot me."

He flashed her a lopsided grin. "I'll do my best."

"I'll be right back."

Annalise doubled back and pecked on the window to the room she and Olivia shared. What were the chances Olivia would respond positively and not automatically assume Annalise was a potential enemy?

The window slid open a crack. "Annalise?"

"Yeah," Annalise whispered. "How did you know?"

"Intruders don't knock." Olivia yawned. "And the men wouldn't have been so gentle."

Good point. But not the point. "We aren't alone, and I smell smoke. Go wake Milt."

Olivia's eyes grew wide. "You don't think . . ."

Annalise nodded. "Fires are the Juarez Cartel's MO."

"If they're trying to scare us out, they're watching the front and back exits."

"Agreed. Get Milt and come through the window. Zach's here with the rifle, but I've got to admit I'm not sure how much good he will be. He's got a nasty wound on his head."

"Stay here." Olivia disappeared into the dark bedroom.

The next breeze brought an even stronger scent of smoke. Where was the fire? Annalise strained her ears listening for sounds of any kind. Everything remained eerily silent except for the wind soughing through the trees. Who was out there? How many were there? What was their intention? Kidnap? Murder? Torture?

The rush of the wind grew louder, followed by popping and cracking. Was the forest itself on fire? Annalise glanced at the sky. A strange orange glow filled the air over the top of the house.

Her stomach dropped to the grass. It wasn't wind she heard. It was the fire consuming the house from the opposite side.

Olivia returned to the window. "The door's too hot to open." Panic filled her round eyes. "What about my dad?"

"We have to get you out of there. Now."

"I can't leave him!"

Annalise's heart ached. "Listen to me. You can't get to him this way."

"But his room is…"

On the opposite side of the house. "I know." Annalise extended her arms. "Come on. I'll help you."

Olivia tucked her gun into her belt and flung her legs over the windowsill. She hesitated and looked over her shoulder. "My dad—"

"You can't help him stuck in your room either, Olivia. Come down. Try to land on your good leg, and I'll support you."

Olivia slid off the sill and jumped to the ground.

Annalise caught her under the arm and helped steady her. This situation couldn't get any better. Two injured officers, one stuck in a burning house, and an unseen enemy. *Lord, where are You?*

She helped Olivia hobble back to Zach. "How're you doing?"

"Dizzy." He grinned.

"Great. You need a hospital." She turned back to Olivia. "You need an orthopedist and complete rest." She sighed. "Milt needs a fireman and…" *We need a miracle.* "Zach, please tell me you have the car keys in your pocket."

He patted his leg. "Yup."

Olivia jerked away. "We can't leave him!" Her fierce hiss barely rose above the noise of the growing fire. It wouldn't be long till the flames broke through the rooms on this side of the house.

"I don't intend to."

Olivia twisted her hands together.

"Come on." Annalise led Zach and Olivia to the edge of the forest and tucked them behind a dense layer of undergrowth. "Keep an eye for whoever has decided to join us. I'll be right back."

"Lise, wait." Zach grabbed her wrist.

She spun to face him. The look on his face said more than any words he could've uttered.

He cleared his throat. "Be careful."

She tried to smile, but it wouldn't form. There was no mirth in the situation or the expression on his face. She pecked him on the cheek. "I will."

Annalise crept back to the house and snuck to the rear corner. She peered into the moonlit back yard. No movement. But that didn't mean someone wasn't hanging in the shadows, waiting for them to show their faces. She would never make it to Milt's window without exposing her position.

Not that it mattered anyway. Flames licked the inside of the panes. If he was in there... She shuddered. Retracing her steps, she peered once more over the porch rails across the front of the house. Though the orange glow from inside the house lit the porch, it didn't seem as intense as the rear.

The porch boards creaked under her weight as she slid under the side rail. "Come on, Milt. Where are you?"

With her back pressed to the front wall, she slid toward the front door. A quick peek through the glass told her there was no entry that direction either. Someone was either hoping to take them out in their sleep or catch them as they ran from the inferno.

What if Milt was already dead? The thought had been trying to come into focus for many minutes. Now it slammed her like a karate kick to the chest.

She had to try. She couldn't just... Annalise grasped the door handle, held her breath, and swung the door in. A blast of desert-like heat rushed into her face. A roar that started at the floor whooshed away from her. Curled upward and met the flames climbing the wall near the staircase. In an instant, the flames touched the ceiling and the flashover poured toward her.

Annalise fell backward, flames leaping above her and igniting the underside of the porch roof in seconds. She scrambled toward the steps, gasping for clean air. That was close. A hot hand gripped her shoulder.

"What are you doing?"

Milt's gruff voice filled her with joy. She sprang to her feet and embraced him. "I thought...I thought you were..."

"Takes more than a little fire to kill a stubborn old guy like me."

She chuckled. "Someone's here. We've got to go." Movement in the corner of her eye caught her attention as she released him. "Milt, duck!" She shoved him to the ground and raised her weapon. Before she could squeeze the trigger, a bullet whizzed by her head, followed by the crack.

Milt rose, grabbed her shoulder, and pulled her toward the side of the house.

Another bullet pinged into the porch somewhere to her left.

"Where are Zach and Olivia?"

Annalise took the lead, racing to the location she'd stashed them. "Guys, time to go."

Zach and Olivia stepped from the underbrush.

Milt spoke over Olivia's shoulder, hugging her tightly. "I don't think we can make the car, Annalise." He directed them all back into the forest. "We need a different plan."

"Fireworks," Zach slurred.

Annalise put her hand on his shoulder. "We aren't at my house, Zach."

"Right." He sank to his haunches and slid the rifle over his knees.

Maybe she should take that from him. He certainly wasn't very lucid. "I don't understand why they aren't just coming at us."

"Me neither," Milt added.

"Maybe it's just a him." Zach looked up at her. "Someone hit me, but I only remember one pair of boots when I hit the ground."

"You mean the Juarez Cartel didn't send the usual army, just one man?" Olivia wrinkled her brow. "Doesn't fit their normal plan of attack."

Annalise shook her head. "I agree."

"That means we have him outnumbered." Zach smiled. "A little distraction, please."

Before Annalise could stop him, Zach raced from their hiding spot toward the front porch. "Zach, wait!" She ran after him. "What's the pla—"

In slow motion, he raised the rifle to his shoulder and fired a round over the top of the porch rail. A handgun report echoed over the roar of the fire now working its way to consuming the entire structure.

She raced to join him. "Zach, it's too hot. This is crazy!"

"Get them to the car."

Annalise tugged on his arm. "Come on, Zach. You're too close!"

He shrugged her off.

She could barely see through the wall of flames to the dark figure on the far side. Why wasn't he opening fire on them both?

Annalise motioned over her shoulder for Milt and Olivia to try to make it to the car parked cattycorner to the porch. If only they had parked twenty feet closer there wouldn't be so much unsheltered space.

She counted down from three to one and then fired three shots in rapid succession.

The man dove for cover.

It was enough for Milt to get Olivia to the car and slip into the rear seat.

"Go, Zach. I'll cover you."

"You go."

"I'm not arguing with you. My eyebrows are about to burn off and my skin is melting. Just go!" She yanked the rifle from his hand and pushed him toward the car.

After a quick reload, she shot at the location she last saw the shadowy figure.

Her SUV came to life and sped toward her with Zach in the driver's seat. That wouldn't work for long. He barely missed the bushes lining the side of the house as he slid to a stop. She yanked the passenger door open and jumped inside. "Go!"

Zach threw it in reverse and flung grass and gravel.

Annalise watched the fireball of a house grow smaller, until it disappeared around a bend in the driveway. Memories of her home and then Paul's burning in much the same manner haunted her.

Had whiskey been used as an accelerant on her home like it had Paul's? Had anyone ever even looked at that? She couldn't remember seeing a report. How had she not noticed that until now?

Olivia had died shortly thereafter. She'd been too focused on solving the mystery surrounding her death. And she would probably never know if one was used here. She would probably have to put a lot of things into that "never know" category, and it killed her.

Zach reached the end of the driveway and whipped onto the road, putting the SUV into drive and squealing the tires as he accelerated. "Where to now?"

"Somewhere to pull over. You can't drive with a concussion."

"Right. Good point."

"I think we need to get to the nearest hospital," Milt said from the back seat. "I'll call Henry and get him to meet us there."

"Why?" Annalise spun in her seat.

Magenta stained Milt's shirt. "It missed my heart, but I . . . can't . . . catch my breath."

Annalise's hand flew to her open mouth and then dropped into a resolute fist. "Pull over, Zach. Now."

She traded seats with him, shoved the car into drive, and took the curves faster than she should. The speedometer didn't drop below fifty until she flew into the Emergency Room drop-off and skidded to a stop.

Chapter Twenty-Four

Zach didn't want to admit it, but his mental clarity wasn't exactly what it should be. He could've sworn he'd just seen Henry out of the corner of his eye. When he turned his head, the image vanished around the corner of the brick hospital. He blinked once, twice. He was imagining that, just like he imagined Annalise sprinting toward him now.

His door yanked open, and he almost fell onto the asphalt.

"Zach, come on, you're next."

Annalise obviously wasn't a mirage. He squinted his eyes. "Huh?" Next for what?

"The ER staff is waiting. I told them we have three injured officers from an undercover operation. They didn't ask more questions. Yet. They will."

She grabbed him under the arm and helped him to his feet. "You need…"

Her mouth continued to move, but he lost ability to hear any of the words. It was as if the entire world was coated in a fuzzy layer of fuzz. He snorted. Clever. Fuzzy layer of fuzz. Was the ground moving under his feet? And why was he tilting so?

Annalise's vice-like grip kept him from slamming into the ground as hard as he would have otherwise. Before his eyes closed, he smiled at the concern on her face. *I love you, Lise.*

Had he said it aloud?

Olivia hugged Milt as the emergency room staff directed him into a wheelchair. "I love you, Dad. Always have."

He smiled weakly. "Always will."

He had no color left in his cheeks, no strength left in the shaky arm he attempted to raise to return her embrace.

Lord, please not my father. Please help him.

They wheeled him through the doors.

She wasn't allowed to follow.

Olivia sank into a chair and propped her throbbing foot into the adjacent one. Her foot ached with each heartbeat, as if the break had a heart of its own trying to escape in the most painful way possible.

A flurry of activity at the front entrance caught her attention.

Nurses pushed someone on a stretcher through, shouting instructions at each other.

Annalise entered behind them with tears streaming down her face.

Olivia jumped onto her good foot and hobbled to embrace her friend. "What happened?"

Annalise sniffled. "He just went down, Olivia. I don't know. I don't know."

"Okay, shh." Olivia patted Annalise's arm. "Calm down, it's going to be okay." She whispered platitudes she didn't feel. Inside, all she could think over and over again was how big of a mess she'd made for everyone. Was her family even safe? Or had she simply endangered them further too?

Tears welled in her eyes. She held Annalise's hand as they both cried.

Annalise swiped at her cheeks. "You should get your foot checked while we are here."

Olivia tried to wiggle her partially exposed toes. They didn't seem to want to respond to her commands. "Yeah, maybe."

"Your toenails don't look normal."

"They are kind of blue, aren't they?" That was probably not a great sign.

"Might as well. It doesn't look like we'll be going anywhere for a while."

She nodded, but that was exactly what was causing the knots in her stomach. If she stayed in one place too long, the Juarez Cartel would find her and her father and friends.

"Come on, I'll sign you in."

Olivia allowed Annalise to direct her to the front desk, but in the back of her mind she was busy formulating an escape plan. Once the doctors fixed her foot, she'd be okay on her own. Her dad would understand. She had to put distance between the walking time bomb of her secret-holding brain and the ones she loved.

"What happened, sir?" the nurse with a grim line for a mouth asked.

"Undercover. Can't give…details." Milt gasped.

"Okay, no more talking."

Thank goodness. Breathing felt like fish hooks yanking a million places inside his chest right now.

They transferred him to a rolling bed. The nurse cut his shirt and undershirt open. Several faces leaned over him, all frowning.

How was he still conscious? He'd managed to never have been shot on the job, but the men and women he'd seen take bullets to the torso went down fast. And didn't get up.

"Prep him for surgery."

"Yes, doctor."

He'd expected as much. "Am I . . ." he couldn't finish the thought. It wasn't his time to go, was it?

The doctor paused and looked directly at him for the first time. "No way to know for sure until we get in there, but I believe the bullet is still in your left lung. You need surgery now to repair the damage."

He nodded, feeling even that small movement in every muscle down to his toes. He was so very tired. His eyes started to slide closed. If he could just rest for a few minutes, everything would be okay.

"Mr. Brooks?"

His eyes snapped open. "Captain."

"Captain Brooks, stay with us, just a few more minutes. Okay?" The nurse was smiling at him again, as she worked to connect the fluids to the fresh IV in his arm.

When had someone put that in? "Tired . . . cold . . ."

The doctor's voice pierced through the closing veil of exhaustion. "One unit of packed red blood cells. Now." He paused. "And take blood samples to see how much more he needs."

Milt didn't care what they did anymore. Fix him. Don't fix him. Just let him sleep. He let his eyelids close. Their voices faded away as the heaviest slumber of his life overtook him.

Annalise tapped her foot on the linoleum floor. How had it only been an hour since Olivia, Zach, and Milt disappeared behind those doors? She'd watched the waiting room ebb and flow with sick people of all ages and diseases, yet she felt so alone she ached. Three of the people she cared most about in this world were just out of reach, just out of her control. The situation had gone from bad to worse and they had no answers. No plan. No chance of winning at the rate they were going.

She dropped her head into her hands. *Lord, seriously. What is Your plan here? I've asked that question so many times over the last year. I can't do this much longer.*

I didn't ask you to, child. Let me handle it all.

Annalise sighed. Same old answer. *I have to help. I have to fix this.*

How?

I don't know, Lord.

Because you aren't in control.

Her fingers trembled as she folded them together. *But I need to be, Lord. You made me this way. Why give me control only to take it away?*

Silence.

All things work together for Your good. She drew a deep breath. *I was never in control, was I? Not of my career, not of my marriage. Not of any of this.*

Now you're getting it.

What do You want me to do?

Nothing.

Ouch. Nothing was harder than everything.

I'll show You when to move. Trust me.

I do.

She sighed and lifted her gaze. Henry stood in the doorway, shifting from one foot to the other. Waiting for her to finish praying, maybe? She flew into his arms. "I am so glad Milt called you. I needed a friendly face."

He cleared his throat and pushed her gently away. "What happened?"

Annalise recapped the past few hours's events. Recalling and rehashing it all drained her a little more with each word.

Henry sat stoically next to her until she finished the discourse. "All three of them are back there somewhere now?"

She nodded.

"Any updates at all?"

"No."

"Sit tight. I'm going to see what I can do. We clearly aren't safe here." Henry disappeared into the darkness outside the emergency room doors.

Annalise sank into the chair, suddenly finding herself more exhausted than she could remember ever feeling before. She laid her head on her hands and let her eyelids slip closed. It felt good to let someone else be in charge right now…

How had Henry gotten here so quickly? When had Milt called him? Annalise searched the jumbled images reeling in her mind's playback. Milt hadn't used his cell phone in the SUV after the house fire. He hadn't even had it in his hand once they arrived at the hospital.

A hand gingerly touched her shoulder.

Annalise jumped as her eyes flew open. "Oh, Olivia, you about scared me half to death."

"Sorry." She smiled. "Like my new cast."

"Oh, purple. Very nice."

"Yeah, the dressing Zach's mom did was cutting off circulation because my leg had swollen so much. It's probably a really good thing you made me get checked out."

Annalise returned her smile. "Good. Sit. We need to make a new plan."

Olivia sat next to her.

"Zach's dad is here. He will be good help." Maybe. Something about his presence bothered her. Why?

Olivia's voice dropped to a whisper. "I almost ran out the back door. I'm endangering all of you just being in the same building."

Annalise took her hand. "We're in this together. I'm ready for the Juarez Cartel to go down once and for all."

"And not get back up."

"Exactly."

Henry entered the front door. His gaze landed on Olivia, and he froze.

Olivia's grip on Annalise's hand tightened.

Annalise glanced at her friend. "You okay?"

Her face paled. "That man . . . we have to get out of here, Annalise."

"That's Zach's father, Olivia. He's on our side."

Olivia grabbed her arm and yanked her to her feet. She left her crutches leaning against the chairs, dragging Annalise through the doors farther into the hospital.

Henry started toward them.

The doors swung closed.

Annalise pulled her friend to a stop. "Olivia, stop. He's here to help."

Olivia shook as she spoke. "Listen to me, Annalise."

"No—"

"Listen. To. Me. I know things, Annalise. You know I do. That man out there may be Zach's father, but he's also the head of the Juarez Cartel."

Annalise chuckled. "Yeah, right, Olivia. Now is not the best time for jokes."

"I'm dead serious. We have to go. If I'm not here, Zach and Milt will be safe. They want me." Olivia charged down the hallway, as fast as she could in a fresh cast.

Annalise chased after her and pulled her around. "What do you know? Why do they want you dead so very badly? You owe me that much." Her heart pounded. "I've lost everything I cared about because of them. Because of you and whatever it is that you are keeping secret. Tell me!" Annalise had gone too far. It certainly wasn't Olivia's fault she'd lost everything, but Olivia was the only one to take her anger out on right now.

"Escape first, talk second." Olivia's eyes widened. "Annalise, please. He's coming."

Annalise glanced over her shoulder. Visible through the windows on the ER doors back to the lobby, Henry moved toward them. "You're sure?"

"Yes."

"Let's go."

Chapter Twenty-Five

Each mile Annalise put between them and the hospital tore a bigger chunk from her heart and threw it to the road to be squashed by her speeding tires. She'd just left Zach. And Milt. The two best friends she had in all the world. "You're sure about this?"

"For the hundredth time, Annalise, yes. I'm sure."

"What if he thinks you told Milt or Zach what you know?" Annalise tossed another frown toward the passenger seat.

Olivia bit her lip. "I don't know."

"Great."

"Look, I'm sorry. I knew this day would come. Somewhere deep inside, I knew it. But all the planning Milt and I did flew out the window when the Juarez guys caught me coming off that Greyhound."

Annalise sighed. Snapping at Olivia, and blaming her for pretty much every bad thing that had ever happened, would do no good. "What was your plan anyway?"

"Step one, disappear and look like a lost hiker."

"You did that marvelously well."

Olivia chuckled. "Thanks. Step two, meet Milt at the restaurant for my new identity. Second one, mind you."

"And? How did that go?"

"I changed the plan before step two."

"Why?"

She glanced out the side window. "Fear, I guess. If no one, not even Milt, knew for sure I was still alive, I thought I could disappear easier. And then if the Juarez Cartel put two and two together and figured out Milt's relationship to me, he wouldn't have information they could torture out of him."

"Smart."

She snorted. "Clearly it's worked so well."

Ouch. Olivia's abrasive tone rubbed Annalise's already flared temper.

"Sorry." She sighed. "Step three was to get on a Greyhound and get as far away as possible. I figured I'd find a way to get a new identity once I made it to Canada or Alaska or Russia."

"How did they find you?"

"They always do, don't they? It took 'em a lot of years this time, but when they want something, they get it."

"If Henry really is who you say, I'm sure the fact that Milt called him in didn't help matters."

"Milt didn't know. I didn't either until they had me at the house, beating me senseless. Henry showed up. I only caught a glimpse of him, but I'm certain. More certain than I've been about anything in this case to date."

"I believe you." Annalise glanced in the rear view, something she'd been doing every few seconds since they had left the hospital. Her breath caught in her throat. Headlights approached quickly. Too quickly. She pressed the pedal harder, and the needle climbed to eighty. The vehicle drew closer, riding up so closely its headlights disappeared from view.

"What is it?" Olivia spun in her seat. "Is that him?"

"I don't know." Annalise changed lanes and the car zipped by on the right. She sighed. "I guess not."

Olivia sighed too.

"Why are we going to Memphis, Olivia? What do they want?"

"Are you sure you want to know?"

"No. But tell me anyway."

"I wasn't just your partner back in Memphis. I was on special assignment. Under Milt's co-direction, along with the Chief of Police. I helped monitor all the potential witnesses against the Juarez Cartel."

"You were a WITSEC handler?"

"Yes. Not a very good one, apparently." She lowered her voice. "I led them right to a young mother. I didn't mean to. I needed to check in with her. We were trying to build a case against them. I visited, thought I was being so careful. Next day, she was dead."

"And her child?"

A tear on Olivia's cheek sparkled in the headlights shining through the windshield. "Yes."

Annalise drew a deep breath.

"I went undercover immediately afterward. Milt hated it. Tried to talk me out of it, but I wouldn't listen."

"That's when they caught you and tried to torture you?"

"Yes. I escaped but just barely. Milt and I knew someone on the inside must be pulling the strings. We just could never figure out who. He helped me fake my death, and well, here we are now."

"The entire Juarez Cartel migrated to Knoxville just to find you?"

Olivia nodded. "They knew it was a cover-up. Somehow. Milt heard rumors through informants for years after my disappearance. When he moved, they did too. It was foolish of us to think we could be near one another and they wouldn't follow."

"Is someone still building a case?"

"Milt has always been building a case. And will until the day he dies."

"Doesn't that mean he's in danger, with Henry in the same hospital as he is?"

"Yes. I'm hoping Henry will take the bait and follow me, though."

"What is the bait?"

"An email I sent to the department director in Memphis."

Annalise groaned. "When exactly did you send this?"

"When we got on the interstate half an hour ago."

"And what did it say?"

"That I am alive and coming back to retrieve the hard copy of the list."

"There's a hard copy?"

"I hid it before I 'died'."

The first sensation Milt was aware of was the scratchiness of his throat. The next, the dull ache in his shoulder. The smells and sounds of the hospital came to life around him as he slowly awoke. Why did his eyelids feel so heavy? He managed to force them open to slits. Other than him and the machines, his room appeared empty. Hard to tell if anyone was on the other side of the blue curtain drawn to his right though.

He tried to scooch up in the bed and immediately regretted the movement when searing pain ripped through his left side. Okay, no moving. Got it.

"Hel-lo?" his whispery voice didn't sound like his own. Okay, no talking. Got it.

So, just lie here until someone arrives? What if they thought he was in a coma and never checked on him until the next shift? He needed a drink. Sooner than next shift. Whenever that may be.

The button! There was always a button. He found the remote next to his right side and pressed all of the buttons with the palm of his hand. A few moments later the door cracked open.

"Mr. Brooks." A red-haired nurse smiled at him from the doorway. "You're awake."

As the door swung wider and the nurse entered, he spotted a man in uniform stationed just outside. What in the world?

"Let's get you some ice chips, Mr. Brooks."

Captain. Captain Brooks. But she was giving him precious liquid for his desert-dry throat, so he could let it slip this time.

She held a spoon to his lips, and he took it like a greedy child in summer with a grape popsicle. "Thank you," he managed to croak out. After another bite of ice, he managed to actually swallow something. "Why . . . officer?"

"Oh, another gentleman was here. Said you all may be in danger and arranged for police protection detail around the clock for your room."

He lifted his eyebrows.

She pointed at the curtain. "You and Officer Leebow."

Milt whipped his head to the right and grimaced. "Open it?"

"I'm sorry, sir, it's against HIPAA policy."

He frowned. "Is he okay?"

"He's in a medically induced coma. Had a subdural hematoma."

"A what?"

"Brain bleed. Doctors are keeping him sedated until they can evaluate the level of swelling on his brain."

"He's my friend. Please?"

She looked over her shoulder to the door. "Oh, all right. But don't tell anyone it was me that opened it, okay?"

"Deal."

Zach's swollen face and bandaged head took Milt's breath. The tubes and wires protruding from every angle weren't pretty to look at either. "Are you sure he's okay?"

"It's too soon to tell. Subdural hematomas are incredibly dangerous. If his brain swells, it could cause irreparable damage."

"Lie to me, why don't you?"

The nurse chuckled. "You strike me as the kind of man who likes truth."

Milt nodded. "Now, about the officer that was here. What'd he look like?"

"Older gentleman, husky voice. Thin. Very serious eyes."

Henry. Milt should've known. Annalise probably called him. "Where is he?"

"Don't rightly know. Haven't seen him since the cavalry outside your door arrived."

Probably chasing down leads. "And the young ladies we came with?"

"I'm sorry, I haven't seen them."

Hopefully, safe with Henry.

The lights of Memphis greeted them with the light of dawn. "We're here."

In the passenger seat, Olivia aroused from sleep and yawned.

"Let's make this quick." Annalise's heart pulled her back to Nashville. To the blonde-haired best friend she desperately needed to make sure was okay. She'd fled without even getting any kind of update. If she called to check, would it somehow tip Henry off?

She cast a sidelong glance toward Olivia. Was she sure she was sure? How could Henry possibly be involved? This was Zach's father, Milt's friend.

But how had he known where to find them?

And would he find Olivia and her before they had a good plan?

"Where to?"

"The library."

How cliché. Annalise chuckled. "Novel idea."

Olivia rolled her eyes.

"Sorry. I'm sleep deprived."

"Let's go retrieve the thumb drive, and then go to the station. If your friend hasn't found us before then."

Annalise groaned. "Lovely thought."

"He always is one step ahead."

"Isn't that the idea this time?"

"Yes, but it still freaks me out."

"You? You're the toughest person I know."

Olivia laughed. "Yeah right. I've been running and hiding for all these years. Real tough."

"Tougher than me," Annalise mumbled.

"Seriously? I always looked up to you, Annalise. You cared about everyone, yet you always kept your head. You figured out stuff even the detectives couldn't see."

She snorted.

"I'm being honest. Why are you so hard on yourself now?"

Because she'd ruined her marriage. Walked away from vows she made before God and her loved ones. Because she couldn't fix Dave. And now she couldn't fix herself. "I don't even know what's broken."

"You can't blame yourself for everything that goes wrong."

"Yes, I can."

"You, my beautiful friend, have no control whatsoever. You know that right?"

"I know it here." She pointed to her head. "Having a hard time accepting it here." She gestured to her heart.

"Pull over." Olivia pointed to an empty curb site.

"What?"

"Now. Pull over."

Annalise did as instructed and turned to her friend.

"We need to pray." Olivia took Annalise's hand and bowed her head. "Lord, we know You are ultimately in control of our lives."

Annalise's heart thumped to life.

"We don't always understand why challenges come, but if we keep our grip on it, our hands in the mix, You aren't free to work. Help Annalise let go of the pain of losing her marriage, of the pain of wondering why it happened. Help her release the guilt and accept the fact that You love her, no matter what. Give her power over her fears."

Sudden tears streamed down Annalise's cheeks. Insecurity. Anger. Guilt. It all stemmed from the fear, didn't it? From the fear she wasn't enough?

"Protect us while we fight these demons that have plagued us for nearly a decade. Bring justice, Lord. Amen."

Annalise squeezed her hand. "Thank you." Olivia's words lifted weight from her heavy heart. For the first time in months, she took a breath that actually reached the recesses of her lungs. The first signs of relief washed over her.

"Ready?"

Chapter Twenty-Six

Olivia led Annalise to the small encyclopedia section of the Cornelia Crenshaw Public Library. She knelt and pulled the Z book from the shelf. *Please let it still be here.* She felt behind the shelf, where dust bunnies fifty years old tickled her fingertips. She bumped something hard and wrapped her fingers around it. *Thank you!*

"Yeah?"

Olivia could sense the unease in Annalise's simple question. "Got it."

"What now?"

"To the station to turn it over to the current handler."

"Isn't he already privy to this information?"

"He thinks he is."

Annalise wrinkled her brow. "I don't understand."

Olivia grabbed her elbow. "Come on, I'll explain on the way. It isn't safe to sit still too long."

At the front exit of the miniscule library, Olivia paused and surveyed the cars in the lot and parked street side. Nothing too suspicious. Yet. She'd chosen this out-of-the-way, hole-in-the-wall place for its unpretentiousness. Apparently, it had worked. The drive had been safe for five years now. Too bad her family and friends weren't.

"I'm listening," Annalise prompted as they walked toward her SUV.

"Dad and I were the only ones who truly knew the identities of every witness. He and I suspected, early into the case, someone on the inside was a member of the Juarez Cartel, so when we had a man in late 2009 who claimed to have witnessed a murder, we hid him. Very, very well."

Annalise unlocked the doors and slid into the driver's seat. "And if they get this, they find him."

Olivia slipped into her seat and shut the door. "Precisely." She sighed. "I've already caused the death of one innocent person. I never want that on my conscience again."

"If you turn this information over, what will stop the Juarez Cartel from getting it and acting?"

Olivia grinned. "Us."

"Lovely."

"Come on, friend. We are tough as nails. Let's show 'em what we're made of." She didn't feel an ounce of the bravado she portrayed. But what choice did she have?

Annalise pulled out of the parking lot. Before she could merge into traffic, a truck slammed into the rear passenger door.

"Hold on!"

Olivia's head bounced against the glass as their SUV slid sideways, the sound of metal crunching louder than an explosion. Hot blood trickled down the side of her face and onto her neck.

Annalise punched the gas pedal and attempted to steer them clear of a second impact.

The truck rammed them and kept pushing, driving them hard off the side of the road.

The SUV bumped over the curb and rocketed into a tree, pinned by the still revving truck. Olivia heard her name being repeated over and over, felt a shake, but couldn't seem to make her body respond. It seemed as though she were looking at everything through an aquarium, the water between her and Annalise's face distorting the images and making them wavy. Nausea threatened to climb into her throat.

"Olivia!" Annalise shook her friend's shoulder for the fourth or fifth time. Pain immobilized Annalise's left arm and leg. She slowly rotated her head, wincing with each fractional movement. The pieces of her shattered window glittered in the brilliant springtime sunshine. The trunk of the tree rested ridiculously close to the side of her head. Where was the rest of her driver's side door?

For a moment, time stood still. The sounds of the impact—the deafening crack of her vehicle's exterior body, the rumbling truck engine, the squeal of tires—filled her mind. Her own engine smoked, hissed, and steamed. Passersby were beginning to stop, to frantically dial 9-1-1 with their cell phones pressed to their heads.

The truck slowly backed up, and a man approached. He reached through the window and grabbed Olivia's ponytail, yanking her head backward. "Where is it?"

Though Annalise's blurred vision couldn't delineate features in the too-bright sunshine, there was no mistaking the voice. Henry Leebow.

"Olivia, tell me where it is. I don't want to have to hurt you."

Annalise snorted. "Already done enough of that, haven't you?" It hurt to move her jaw. It hurt worse to realize Zach's father was trying to kill them. And had probably done it multiple times before.

Henry's gaze remained fixed on Olivia, "Hello, Annalise. Hush, now. It'll be over soon."

Over? Permanently? She had no doubt that was his intention. She slowly released her seatbelt and slid her weapon from its holster, the movements shielded by Olivia's body sitting ten inches closer to her than she would've normally, before her vehicle was squashed like a discarded tissue.

She would get one chance at this. One. *Lord, help me.* "It's in her right pants pocket. Just take it and leave her alive. She doesn't have a clue what's happening right now."

"Yeah, right." Henry chuckled. "Leave no witnesses has always been my motto."

"What about all these people?"

Henry's gaze jerked to the crowd forming nearby. His face paled.

Annalise took the opportunity to lift her gun and train it on his chest. "You got sloppy. It took way too long, but you got in too big of a hurry."

"No matter." He returned his gaze to Annalise and smiled. "You won't shoot me. It would break my son's heart to know the woman he loved murdered his father." Henry made a move to reach for Olivia's pocket.

"Don't do it."

"Listen, Annalise, either shoot me or stop pretending." He dug into Olivia's pocket, retrieved the thumb drive, and then pulled a knife from his belt. He brought it to Olivia's throat.

At the sight of the first drop of bright red blood, Annalise squeezed the trigger. The sound exploded inside her vehicle, adding to the ringing she already had from the wreck.

Henry dropped instantly out of view.

The dull thump made Annalise's stomach turn. Tears sprang to her eyes. "You were wrong, Henry." On so many levels.

Chapter Twenty-Seven

Annalise's and Olivia's hospital stay felt interminably long. Each with concussions, multiple broken bones, and new Frankenstein stitches, they made quite the pair as they hobbled out of Baptist Memorial Hospital four days later. Annalise itched to get back to Nashville. To Zach and Milt. She needed to lay eyes on them to believe they were okay.

Henry's body would be left behind. Retrieved later should Zach decide to do so. How was she going to explain everything that happened?

She'd updated Kirk, and he'd made sure the officers guarding the men were trustworthy. He'd also helped get Lorraine home and given updates to everyone waiting at home.

The drive back to Nashville seemed even longer. Hadn't Annalise lectured Zach just a few days prior about not driving with a concussion? And now here she was doing exactly that. The farther from Memphis they got, the more everything that had happened began to feel like a dream. She had shot Zach's father. Killed him. She shuddered. Tears welled every time she thought about it. About the fact that Zach would never get the closure he needed now. Would never have all the answers he sought. The relief of taking out the head of the Juarez Cartel couldn't overcome the hurdle of the guilt and grief she felt.

Olivia slept most of the drive, leaving Annalise alone with her torturing thoughts. As she pulled into the hospital parking lot, she nearly turned around. Her racing heart wanted her to flee, but her conscience dragged her inside, a groggy Olivia hobbling at her heels. Neither one of them seemed to have words on the elevator ride up to Milt and Zach's room.

Annalise nodded at the officer at the door and gently pushed the door open. Her breath caught as her gaze landed on Milt. He sat in his bed, quietly reading a magazine. And looking exactly like his same old self. *Thank you, Lord!*

Olivia squeezed past her and ran to her father's side.

He dropped the magazine and wrapped Olivia in a long embrace.

Annalise's gaze traveled farther into the room and landed on Zach. In stark contrast, he lay motionless and flat in the bed, with thick, white bandages covering his hair. She couldn't move. Could scarcely breathe. How could she have left him in this state? How could she have gone days without an update and not even known how bad it was?

Somehow, her feet carried her to his side. She sank onto the bed next to him and let the tears fall. She felt Milt and Olivia's gazes on her, but they remained silent. Slowly, she leaned over him and placed a gentle, long kiss on his forehead. Would he ever do that again to her? She'd taken everything about him for granted far too long, and now—she choked back a guttural sob.

A warm hand pressed against her cheek.

Her eyes flew open as she jerked backward.

Zach grinned up at her, his thumb still stroking her cheek. "Everything okay?"

"You...I thought you were—"

"Just sleepin'. Killer headache, but the docs say I'll be fine. I'm too stubborn to die, you know."

Annalise gently slapped his shoulder. "You scared me half to death."

Zach pulled her face closer. "I'll be okay. You, however, are looking a little rough."

She chuckled. "Gee, thanks."

"Care to tell me the story?"

Annalise's heart sank. Confession time. Would he still love her in any capacity when she finished?

She leaned back, and his hand dropped to hers, resting on the bed next to him. Annalise glanced at Olivia, who similarly sat with Milt.

Olivia nodded.

The rock in her stomach seemed to occlude words for a moment. But with Zach's next flashing broad grin, she related all that had happened over the past twenty-four hours. Everything spilled out in a near-breathless, run-together stream of words and tears.

Zach's face paled, his smile slipping away.

She was breaking his heart! And that was breaking hers. "Zach, I'm so, so sorry. I don't know how you'll ever forgive me."

The following seconds stretched into agonizing moments. Was he ever going to speak? Was her heart going to keep beating until he did?

"This isn't your fault, Lise. There's nothing to forgive."

"Wait. What?"

"You heard me. You did your job, and I'm proud of you." He smiled and tugged on her arm. "Closer."

She leaned in, expecting a kiss to the forehead, like usual.

He placed his hand on her cheek once more and directed her lips to his.

Fireworks and bombs and sparklers and everything else noisy and beautiful and glittery exploded inside her, ricocheting to every part of her body. Whoa.

When he pulled away, Annalise couldn't open her eyes. Not even if she'd wanted to.

"I love you, Lise. Not just as friends."

It took a full thirty seconds for her to find her voice. She swallowed hard and peeled her daydream-heavy eyelids open. "I love you too, Zach."

He sighed. "Oh, thank heavens. That would've been super embarrassing if you'd said I was crazy."

She laughed, but he interrupted it with another fiery kiss.

So, this is what it felt like to fall in love with your best friend, huh? Annalise thought she might be able to get pretty used to it, pretty quickly. She smiled as a future she could once more look forward to returned to focus.

Chapter Twenty-Eight

Olivia paused on her front step, drew a deep breath, and sent up a silent prayer of thanks. He had brought her home. Her husband and babies waited just inside. Two days ago, she was sure she'd not see them again until they met in heaven.

She swung the door open and hobbled inside. Time stood still as her gaze locked with Jonah's.

His eyes widened. His jaw dropped.

Tears clouded her vision. "Hi."

Without a word, he stumbled over the toys in the floor and wrapped her in his safe, strong arms. Home. She was finally home.

"Mom?" Andi's shaky voice asked from nearby.

Olivia opened her eyes.

Jonah released his grip.

The crutch she held under her arm fell to the floor, and both children raced to wrap her waist with their little arms. "Oh, I missed you both so much. I'm so, so sorry." She squeezed them as hard as her one semi-good arm would allow.

"What happened to you?" Drew asked.

"It's a long story. But what you really need to know is that it's over." And if she had anything to say about it she wasn't going anywhere ever again.

The next day after arriving home, Milt pulled to a stop in front of the Motel 6.

Orrin waited, leaning against the railing, arms crossed over his chest. Pants sagging a mile.

They'd have to discuss those britches at some point. Milt leaned out the window. "Get in the truck." He gave Orrin a look he hoped said he meant business.

Orrin didn't argue.

Milt started the truck as Orrin sat down and slammed the door. "Put your seatbelt on, boy."

Again, Orrin complied in silence.

"We need to have a chat."

Silence.

"Your brother is doing great. He doesn't need trouble from you. You understand me?"

Orrin grumbled his reply.

"You will address me as sir, as your brother does. Understood?"

Orrin hesitated but finally mumbled, "Yes, sir."

Maybe there was hope for the young man after all. "I'm gonna tell you a story, and I expect you to take it seriously. You hear me?"

"Yes, sir."

"I lost everything that was important to me. My wife, my kids, my home. Twice. Everything but my job because I was stubborn and made poor decisions. My girl Olivia is back to me by miraculous circumstances."

"Why's this matter to me?"

"You wait till I'm done, you'll find out." Milt sighed. "I've made a lot of mistakes. What I'm about to offer ain't going to make up for all of them, but helping your brother has made me happier than I've been in a decade. If you think you can abide by my rules, like he has, you're welcome to stay with me. As long as you need."

Orrin's gaze jerked to him, jaw dropped. "Why would you do that?"

"Because I love your brother, and he loves you."

"What're the terms?"

"You go to rehab. You complete rehab." Milt pinned him with a stern glare. "That's a deal breaker. If you leave without completing the program, you're out."

Orrin nodded, almost imperceptibly.

"When you get out, you get a job and you work as hard as you can to provide for yourself and your brother."

"All right."

"And you come to church at least once a week with me. You don't have to love it or even believe it, but I want you to see it before you decide."

Orrin was silent for a full five minutes before softly replying, "Okay."

"This is the only second chance you'll get from me. Don't take it for granted."

"Yes, sir."

Milt pulled to a stop at the next red light and extended his hand. "Men shake on deals and don't go back on their word."

Orrin hesitated and then squeezed Milt's hand in a firm grip. "Yes, sir."

Zach leaned his hip against Kirk's desk, folded his arms across his chest, and smiled.

Kirk stood across from him, grinning. "Good job, guys. You two really do make a good team."

Annalise smiled.

Zach aimed his smile at her, and a blush crept into her cheeks. Could he be any prouder of her? He doubted it. "I have a question, Kirk."

"Shoot."

"Any policy against Special Agents dating?"

Kirk's eyebrows shot up, and Annalise's blush deepened.

"Zach!"

"Well, I need to know."

Kirk glanced from him to Annalise and back again. An even bigger grin settled on his lips. "Not a one. Congratulations."

"Thanks." The pride Zach felt in his beautiful best friend turned girlfriend filled his chest with a warm, full-to-the-brim sensation. "It's gonna be our best teamwork yet."

Annalise smacked his biceps, but she nodded along with his idea. He had a long way to go toward moving past the grief of his dad, toward forgiveness for someone who he could never speak to again, and he couldn't imagine a better partner—on the job or in life—than Special Agent Annalise Raven Baker.

The End

Dear Readers,

I hope you have enjoyed continuing Annalise and Zach's story.

Check out book number three, *The Drowning of Corinne Porter*, which is available for preorder on Amazon soon! Coming June 2021!

When an unreliable witness reports a body that they can't find…

Special Agents Annalise Baker and Zachary Leebow will be stretched to the limits of their patience and their imaginations. Deep in the wilderness of Cades Cove, the Smoky Mountain Investigate Force's spotless track record is on the line if they fail.

…But how do they solve a crime when there is no victim?

Pssst.. Just a quick reminder, if you haven't already, please join my newsletter. I'd love to have you! Sign up now and get my free eBook novella, *Of Walls*, delivered right to your inbox. Plus get the inside scoop on all of my new releases and giveaways and receive monthly newsletters where we can connect, get to know each other, and pray for one another. Here is the link (or click on the image below): http://eepurl.com/cfqP5H

Acknowledgments

Thank you—You know who you are. My family is amazing. My Lord is amazing. I am blessed.

About the Author

Sara is a multi-published, award-winning author and mother of five who writes surrounded by the beauty of East Tennessee. She earned her bachelor's degree in Animal Science from the University of Tennessee and is a member of American Christian Fiction Writers. She is the author of the Love, Hope, and Faith Series, which includes *Callum's Compass* (2017), *Camp Hope* (2018), and *Rarity Mountain* (2019). She also has a story, "Leap of Faith," in *Chicken Soup for the Soul: Step Outside Your Comfort Zone* and a novella, *Of Walls* (2018). Sara finds inspiration in her faith, her family, and the beauty of nature. When she isn't writing, you can find her reading, camping, and spending time outdoors with her family. To learn more about her and her work or to become a part of her email friend's group, please visit www.saralfoust.com.